MEL'S ITALIAN PROJECT

SIMON POTTER

Trans-Oceanic-Press

2024

"Melyssa's Italian Project" was first published in Great Britain by **_Trans-Oceanic-Press_** 2024

Copyright © Simon Potter

Simon Potter has asserted his right under the Copyright, Designs and Patents Act, 1988, to be identified as the author of this work.

www.simonpotterauthor.com

ISBN: 978-1-9164295-6-7

A catalogue record for this book is available from the British Library.
Cover by Gingernut Designs

The novel is a work of fiction. Any resemblance to actual persons, living or dead, is entirely coincidental.

This book is sold subject to the condition that it shall not, by way of trade or otherwise, be lent, re-sold, copied, or circulated without the publisher's prior consent in any form of binding or cover other than that in which it is published.

Printed and bound by Witley Press, Hunstanton, Norfolk, PE36 6AD

"If you prick us, do we not bleed?"

(Shakespeare: The Merchant of Venice)

NEWS

For the third night in a row Melyssa awoke in the grip of a nightmare about the black shape above her. She sat up, gasping, and stared into the spangly darkness, aware that she had cried out.

'Melyssa!' It was her mother's voice from across the small landing. Slippered footsteps came to Melyssa's door. There was a tap. 'Melyssa, girl? You were shouting out. Can I come in?'

Mrs Mosengo gingerly opened her daughter's bedroom door and stood framed in the light from her own room.

'Oh!' gasped Melyssa. 'Come in, Mum. A horrid dream. I'm all right now.'

Melyssa switched on the bedside light and composed her features.

'You were shouting,' said her mother, half-accusingly, half-anxiously. 'That's every night since you've been back home. I knew it was a mistake you going and joining T-ray. It was all too much for you with things so bad at the moment.'

Melyssa sighed.

'Mum, T-ray and I are all right. We have this conversation every time I come home. T-ray can cope in London because he's a man. I should stay in Bristol because I'm a girl. Things are difficult now, I know. First Brexit, then Covid, now cost of living. You think I'm suffering from mental stress, or whatever, but I don't think that even the strain of running a design shop is going to carry us off with heart-attacks. No, it's just my dreams. I've had a nightmare, and I…'

Melyssa found her voice drying up. She had nearly told her mother about the black shape. But it seemed silly speaking about it now she was awake – and it gave it a reality she did not want it to have.

'I'm going to make a nice cup of tea,' said Mrs Mosengo, and she flip-flopped off downstairs to the kitchen. 'And you need a digestive biscuit,' she called back. 'You don't eat enough. You never have.'

Left alone, Melyssa shook the dark image from her brain.

'It's stupid,' she muttered, half-aloud, as though to convince an unseen listener. ' "The horror of the semi in Castleton Road." Perhaps Mum's right – my blood sugar is low.' Not for the first time she framed the intention to have a health check-up when back in London.

Despite her dismissal of her mother's anxieties, no one was more conscious than Melyssa of the strain of the last year. She had happily acquiesced when T-ray had suggested they become partners in his fledgling design set-up in Battersea. She had amused both her brother and her father when she had revealed that she did not really know where in London Battersea was. 'You provincial girls,' they had laughed. T-ray had warned her that life was going to be far from easy.

'It's hardly the big-time, you know. There's thousands of people like us. I expect a big struggle to get established. And – you know – it's not an obvious field for POC guys like us. I think we'll see prejudice. But then I've got the training and you've always been real good at design. Beats me why you didn't go into it after your degree. I never thought you'd stick at the teaching art bit for so long.'

For some moments his shrewd eyes had taken in the lines of discontent forming round Melyssa's mouth. 'Better to be Miss Broke of Battersea than Miss Bugger-All of Bristol.'

There are no flies on T-ray, thought Melyssa. He had always been quick to see the truth. Pulling her duvet round her chin, she recalled the mixture of guilt and relief she had felt when she had handed in her notice at school, packed her bags, reassured her parents and severed ties with the city in which she had lived for twenty-eight years. She had hardened herself to ignore Mrs Mosengo's hurt expression whenever her daughter's discontent with her home and routine became especially acid during those six weeks when she worked off her remaining contract. She was, she told herself, only asserting her right to independence. She was aware that she had grown away from her mother in particular during her time in Battersea, but she was a long way from realizing what a hard shell she had developed. Sometimes, when she had instances of how much she had changed, she justified it by admitting that life had, as T-ray warned, been tough. She needed a shell to survive, and today's bright black woman had to be business-like. Sentiment was for kids. So – if it came to that – were ridiculous nightmares.

'Just coming, dear,' called her mother from below.

Yet the nightmare is so real. That dark cone of a hill, the heat, insects humming and against the sky the black shape. Oh, its height! And those rushing clouds! She drew up her knees and pillowed her chin on them. Her eyes hardly saw her mother come in with the tea tray.

Morning, and the early summer sun was pink in Melyssa's room. By her bed her smartphone was tinkling with her special jingle. She grabbed it up.

'T-ray! What is it? What's happened? It's so early.'

'Jeez, it's hardly the crack of dawn, Mel. I called Mom, and she says you've been snoring fit to burst after a disturbed night. Lucky someone in this outfit is up and doing some work. I've got news for you. Want to guess?

'Oh, um, yes. Don't tell me. Well, I suppose it's a job, isn't it?'

'It's a job. Yup.'

'A dining-room? In Chelsea?'

'Guess again.'

'More than a room?'

'More.'

'Gosh. Not a house? Don't say we've at last got a whole house to do! Where? Whose? How much?' Melyssa turned her mind to the welcome economics of the good news. 'How much? What are they paying?'

'You ain't guessed right, sister,' laughed T-ray. 'Keep on. You'll get there – perhaps.'

'So it's not a house? Oh, don't tell you've rung up just to tell me that someone's called in and bought a tapestry cushion, or one of our lights.'

'It's a theatre.'

'A what?'

'A thee-ay-ter. You know, where they put on plays. Or, to be precise in this case, where they put opera on.'

'And we're designing what bits of it? Not stage sets, surely? I haven't done anything for the stage since my one go at uni.'

'No, no. Everything BUT the stage. It's a restoration job, see? A huge job,' cried T-ray, his voice light-sounding with happiness. 'It's our big break.'

'How wonderful. If you think we can do it, that is. "Calypso Designs" on to the big time at last. When am I needed?'

'Get a train back today. We've got people to meet tomorrow morning. Tell Mum we'll come and see her and Dad before we go. Bye, Mel.'

T-ray was about to ring off, but Melyssa's shriek arrested him in time.

'Stop!' she cried. ' "Before we go" you said. Before we go where?'

'Oh, sorry,' said T-ray. 'I should have mentioned it earlier. This theatre isn't in the UK at all. It's in Italy, and it's called – er, hang on, I've got it written down somewhere – er, Torre Del Purgatorio. It's near Lucca, between there and Montecatini Terme. Chiantishire, doncha know! A lot of ex-pat well-to-do toffs there. Wait 'til they see us!'

There was a click. T-ray had gone.

Melyssa took a deep breath. She thought she had better wait to tell both her parents the news. She hoped her father would be coming home for lunch.

"That was T-ray, I suppose,' said her mother. "Time to go back to Battersea. Is that what the call was?"

"He does think I ought to get a train today, Mum. He's got an important client for us to meet early tomorrow.'

'A short visit again,' muttered Mrs Mosengo, 'and off overdoing it and getting stress nightmares. I do wish you were still teaching at Fenthorpe.

A steady job, a pension if you go back to it after your own children are grown up, a bit of respect from people....' Her voice trailed away. Melyssa looked quite steely for a moment.

'Yes, Mum, I know. And why didn't I go steady with Brian Lockley at the Law Courts? And why didn't I marry him and already have two point four kids? And why aren't I living at 36. Castleton Road. So handy being just round the block. God, Mum, you sound like someone in *Coronation Street* circa 1975 sometimes.'

Mrs Mosengo's face looked so woebegone as she turned away to get her daughter "a good breakfast" that Melyssa relented, jumped up and hugged her impulsively. She wondered what had prompted her to speak so cruelly. She knew well enough that life had not been easy for her mother, that Mrs Mosengo made sacrifices and expected no return. It was just that her mother's aspirations for her seemed so unexciting. Over a year in London in a milieu different from that of her upbringing had changed Melyssa too much for her to have patience with her mother. Exactly why Mrs Mosengo spoke like someone in a Talking Pictures 1960s black and white film, Melyssa did not know. Her mother was only just over fifty and coped well with her job in a building society office. Dad made enough from his insurance sales. Neither was a kill-joy fogey.

When the breakfast arrived, Melyssa decided she would tell her mother T-ray's news.

'Eat the eggs before they get cold,' said Mrs Mosengo, pouring tea.

'Look, I'm sorry, Mum,' said Melyssa. 'The news T-ray told me is that "Calypso Designs" are going to get a commission to do up a whole theatre. In Italy too! Doesn't that sound exciting?'

Yet even while her mother was nodding, the name of their destination came back to her. Torre del Purgatorio. For one inexplicable moment she was filled with the terror of her nightmares.

At the station Melyssa bumped into the girl who had been her closest school friend. This sort of thing was always happening. It was one of the reasons she disliked going back to Bristol.

'How's things?' asked Rebecca in her soft West-country tones.

'Fine. Thanks. Super,' replied Melyssa, feeling that she was overdoing the Chelsea-ish was of speaking she had adopted. As Rebecca obviously expected it, she asked, 'What are you doing here at the station?'

'Seeing mum-in-law off – she's on her way home to Leeds. You're quite the stranger here now. Busy in London, I expect?'

'Absolutely.'

'My little someone's at her nursery now,' continued Rebecca. 'And Joseph will be four in September. Would you believe it?'

'Oh, yes. I mean, no. Gosh,' said Melyssa. She hadn't remembered what Rebecca's eldest was called – nor whether it was male or female, nor how old it was.

'What have you been up to then?' asked Rebecca. The platform indicator clicked round to let passengers know which platform the Paddington train was on. Melyssa made a move to the barrier.

'Why, I'm taking "Calypso Designs" to Italy to do design work for a theatre in a few days,' said Melyssa rather grandly.

'Italy, eh?' replied Rebecca, who was nothing like as dumb as Melyssa took her for. 'Quite like old times then, isn't it?' Melyssa gazed at her sharp face. 'The Great Italian Romance, in your last year at the uni, remember?'

'I'm not sure I can remember it was quite as you put it,' snapped Melyssa as the barriers opened.

'I can. Even though it's seven years ago. I'll see you off.'

Melyssa boarded the train after the briefest of goodbyes. Too late, she wished she had squandered money on a first-class ticket, instead of letting Rebecca see her enter second-class.

'Goodbye, Mel. I must go and get my husband's dinner,' said Rebecca. It seemed to Melyssa that she had emphasised the word "husband" and had twisted her wedding-ring under Melyssa's eyes. 'Be seeing you, I expect.'

The train began to flash east and Melissa squirmed in her seat.

How typical to meet Rebecca just this morning when I was beginning to feel happy again, she thought. And how typical of her to drag Angelo up again. God, it's more awful every time I come back. Well, I won't think about it – I just won't.

But as the rails unwound, she could not help herself thinking about that disastrous affair with her mature student, her mother's tears, her father's threats, Angelo's Catholic family nearly carrying her to the altar. How glad she was when Angelo graduated and left for Milan. Those embarrassing love-makings. Poor Angelo, all those years a mummy's boy and being expected to satisfy an ardent girl ten years younger. Yet he had established or confirmed, perhaps, Melyssa's inner standard for men – an archetype she carried round inside her. He had been older, was dark-skinned and he wasn't from Somerset. And oh, that terrible evening in his bedroom when, making love, they had thought his mother was out – and she hadn't been. And the break-up, with him in tears. And then, a year later Brian, her mother's knight-in-shining-armour for her daughter on the rebound. The sum total of my romantic life.

She felt herself going hot and cold when she recalled the tone that Rebecca used in her comment about Italians. It was all very well for Rebecca to be superior, but I, thought Melyssa, have a career, a business, a future. I'm not going to be imprisoned in Bristol before I'm thirty, putting a man's socks out for him and slaving in a little semi.

'Have you heard,' asked T-ray, as he and his sister walked arm-in-arm across the Albert Bridge, 'of a top cat called Emilio Monza?'

'I certainly have,' replied Melyssa, amused, but exasperated at his assumption that she probably hadn't. 'God, T,' she went on, 'You really mustn't class me in the same boat as those dumb, directors-lunch-preparing, Peter-Jones-shopping dolly-birds you're so keen to get in touch with nowadays.'

'Okay, just business. Cool, big sis. I only mentioned this Monza because he's the guy with the Italian project.'

Since she had met T-ray at The Chelsea Arts Club to have a drink after her train journey, Melyssa had pestered him with questions about the Great Italian Job. It was odd, now she stopped to think about it, that he hadn't mentioned the man behind it until now.

T-ray grinned at his sister. She was clearly impressed.

'Emilio Monza! That's pretty exciting. You mean you've *met* him?'

Monza did not seem the sort of person ordinary people met. Like his countryman, the late Pavarotti, he seemed, to Melyssa's mind, what a celebrity should be: magnetic, attractive, but unapproachable.

'He came to the shop in Battersea.'

'I can't believe it!' Inside, Melyssa was still unsophisticated enough to find such a thing thrilling. It was why she had left Bristol.

'Yup. He and his dishy cousin dropped by. Yes, my girl,' he went on waspishly, correctly divining her naïve enthusiasm, 'He actually sat upon the same chair which your own fair bum has graced. We must never dust it again.'

'Idiot,' laughed Melyssa, undecided whether to be cross with him. She lifted her hand to her black curls and pushed them back as the wind off the Thames ruffled them.

'You shouldn't do that, you know,' remarked T-ray. 'You're too keen on plastering your mane back and pinning it. It makes you look too prim and severe, like a librarian. You've got lovely Afro hair. Let it fluff out free.' He reached out and lifted its shape with his fingers.

'Stop it, you twit!' she cried, irritated, but pleased by the compliment. 'Really, T, I don't know what's got into you today. Sewing up huge contracts, meeting celebs, telling your big sister how to bob her hair, being so cagy about Monza. Yes, *why*,' she said, 'has it taken you two hours to tell me that Calypso is contracted to one of the greatest opera stars in the world? Why did you leave me wondering if we were signing up with Pope Francis, Fiat or a pizza chain. Why the mystery?'

T-ray seemed taken aback by her direct questioning.

'Oh, well, nothing, really,' he stammered. 'It was just, just part of the deal, you see.'

'No, I don't see. What was part of what deal?'

'Part of our restoration deal for that theatre, of course.'

'Yes, yes, but *what* was this mysterious part of the deal?' hooted Melyssa, alarmed at her brother's secretiveness and wondering if he had landed Calypso in some sort of unbreakable contract – a clash with the Mafia, perhaps, which was going to leave them penniless.

'If you must know, the theatre deal is only on providing *you* go to Italy to do the work. It's not enough, apparently, for us to do designs in London and get them over to Lucca, nor is it enough for me to go on my own, or to send Joe or even Alice, if we use her again. Signor Monza said it had to be *you* on the job, or nothing. *You* or no job. He was most insistent. I – I did think it was a bit odd,' added T-ray in self-defence, 'especially as you'd never met him before. I mean how could you have done? And where had he heard about the firm? It can't have been through that conservatory in Wimbledon, or the games room in Fulham, can it?'

Melyssa was stunned. She walked on to the end of the bridge, wondering what it all meant.

'T,' she said, as they passed Foxmore St, 'are you telling me that such a big name in opera today – up there with Andrea Boccelli – the man who did Central Park, packed out the O2, made a Verdi song a hit in the charts, has millions of followers on-line, has specifically picked out Calypso Designs of Battersea run by you and yours truly out of all the great design houses in the world from La Chanterelle and Ghia through Colefax, Richardson, Neumann's and the Triangle in the USA? Has gone specially to 37a Bridge Place to an utterly untried concern run by two nobodies from Bristol? Why?'

'Oh, no, c'mon…..'

'Let me finish,' snapped Melyssa. 'He has gone to the "Have-you-an-oak-lavatory-seat-please" end of the market purely because he wants me, Mel Mosengo, and you, T-ray Mosengo, neither of whom he's never met, never heard of, never likely to have heard of, to go and work in Torre di Whatever on a huge theatre restoration and re-design. Is he mad?'

'I don't *know* why, I tell you!' shouted T-ray. 'It's what he said. I know it sounds peculiar; it *is* peculiar – but do you really think I'd turn down the contract we've been praying for because of a little oddness, did you?'

Melyssa hardly knew what to say. What *was* there to say?

'Do I get to meet him too?' she asked.

'Of course. Of course. He's staying at The Dorchester. He wants to meet up tomorrow. In fact he wanted to get together today, but I told him you'd gone to see Mum. He's amazingly keen and – and really quite a nice guy.'

'Liar,' said Melyssa, with a sister's directness. 'You don't like him.'

'Well, he's a touch overbearing close-to,' admitted T-ray, wrinkling his nose. 'But his cousin's a bit of all right! Wait 'til you meet her!'

His eager face broke into a wide smile. Melyssa stepped to his side and hugged him.

'I'm sorry. I'm being a bitch. I should be congratulating you instead of snapping and questioning. It's just that I've had a bloody awful day, all in all, and a bad night last night. I think you've been wonderful. I really do. The best brother in the whole world!'

'Hey, that's better, Sis,' smiled T-ray, grateful that one of their rare quarrels had not developed out of the discussion. 'You wait. You'll like him. You'll see.'

But that night, in her room round the corner from the design studios where T-ray lived, Melyssa had the most terrifying of all her many recent dreams of the black tower. She was looking up a conical hill in a hot, dry night. She couldn't move onto the heavy, steep steps that led up to lighted windows under the dark shape. Electrical flashes were playing about the low clouds. The last thing she saw on awakening, sweating, was the tower opening and tentacles reaching down to drag her in. This after-image remained with her all morning.

'Piacere, Signorina,' said the glamorously dressed Italian woman, of whom T-ray had spoken, in response to Melyssa's greeting.

Melyssa had come into the Dorchester's pillared lobby where T-ray lay at ease in a deep chair. He and she had spent more than two hours with a solicitor and now, feeling almost like a groupie, Melyssa was waiting to greet the great man. Signor Monza was not staying at the hotel alone, for the brother and sister had met four different people before Contessa Frosinone, appeared and introduced herself to Melyssa.

'How do you do,' had murmured Melyssa. Even so long after the Covid catastrophe, she still hesitated about shaking hands with strangers. But the Contessa merely nodded and then looked across at T-ray.

'I like to come to London at this time of year. When *mio marito* – my husband, the count – was alive, we used to take a house, *una barraca*, in Scotland to entertain. This is why my English is not too bad, I think.'

'It's excellent!' cried T-ray, all attention to the Contessa's lightest word, 'but I didn't know that Italians visited Scotland.'

'Ma certo,' smiled the Contessa. 'All the time. It is a favourite destination – the highlands – because they are *freddo,* cold. Nice and cold. We are always too hot – and it gets worse because of the climate change, I think.'

T-ray grinned with full wattage at her. Melyssa studied her covertly. She must have been widowed very young, or married Count Frosinone very early. Melyssa thought that she was not more than a couple of years older than herself. She didn't like her much, but honesty compelled her to admit that she was spectacular. T-ray was obviously charmed by her and, in consequence, was ignoring his sister.

The Contessa was strikingly dressed in black, with dramatic red accessories and much gold jewellery. Melyssa, though confident about her own clothes, did feel dimmed by the aura of theatrical wealth exuding from the Italian. After the brief greeting the young widow ignored her and spoke exclusively to T-ray, from which Melyssa deduced that she despised other women, particularly when men were present. Melyssa also had a strong feeling that the Contessa didn't really have much regard for, or interest in, her brother. A seam of insincerity ran through most of what she said – although T-ray, the poor slob, clearly didn't notice.

Suddenly there was a stir in the hotel lobby. Two or three girls and a few middle-aged women who had been hovering uncertainly near the entrance darted forward into the pillared area. Emilio Monza had arrived from his suite upstairs. Heads turned to see what was going on. There was a shout and a further half-dozen people came in from Park Lane, pursued by doormen. They surged round Signor Monza, waving their smartphones to get selfies.

Emilio stooped among them – he was tall for an Italian – and let himself be photographed. Someone seized his hand and shook it. A girl reached up to kiss his cheek while her friend's phone snapped them. At this, the hotel staff came forward and ushered the fans outside. Emilio turned from them to face the pillared area where T-ray, Melissa and the Contessa awaited him. Coming towards them, he acknowledged their greetings. Melyssa could see that he was profoundly aware of the eyes of others on him. On television, which is where she herself had seen him, his hair, black with gold tints, his strong oval face and white teeth had made her believe that he was beautiful. Now he came close to her, she was disconcerted by his size, his muscular body and by his enormous confidence and self-awareness. This then was charisma, stage presence – the aura of stardom.

'Hello again,' cried T-ray, leaping up. 'This is really kind of you asking us to dinner. My sister and I are thrilled. I was just telling your cousin that we do feel a piece of good fortune has come our way, and that we will do our best to fulfil your expectations.'

Oh, stop it! Stop it! groaned Melyssa inwardly. Her brother's gush sounded so grovelling. At that moment she despised him: the small business owner saying anything to keep the latest client. Outwardly, she kept a smile going, watching Emilio Monza's face as she did so. The celebrity singer was nodding calmly, his well-kept hand clasping T-ray's. Contessa Frosinone had changed expression and looked sulky and scowling for an instant. No one but Melyssa seemed to have noticed and it passed so quickly that she wondered whether she had imagined it.

'Emilio, *caro,*' purred the young widow, taking the singer's hair in her red-varnished nails. She pulled his head down, raised her predatory mouth and kissed the famous singer full on the lips. T-ray looked very put out. Melyssa felt a slight revulsion.

'Loredana, *per favore,* no....', murmured Emilio. Can they be lovers? thought Melissa, surely not. It's just her stupid manner. He objected, didn't he?

'Mr Mosengo, what a pleasure to see you tonight. We must talk more about our great plans over dinner. And I am most delighted to meet you at last, *Signorina*,' he added, turning his full attention upon Melyssa for the first time.

Without being able to explain why, but feeling that it was partly a result of her brother's fulsomeness, partly a ridiculous jealousy at the thought of Loredana Frosinone as Emilio Monza's lover, and partly because her latent sense of inferiority and insecurity – both racial and economic – was made defensive and prickly in the presence of riches and fame, Melyssa became sharp and graceless. She hardly acknowledged his greeting. She felt a heat creep into her cheeks as he gazed at her closely. Is he interested in me? she wondered; or is he comparing me unfavourably with that – that bitch?

Then Emilio Monza smiled and turned back to T-ray.

'Come, you must be hungry. I certainly am. This cool London air gives me an appetite.'

During that meal, Melyssa felt that she had seldom appeared to less effect. Loredana, by contrast, sparkled in a loud and demanding way, constantly patting either Emilio's or T-ray's arms, and flashing brilliant smiles on them both. Typical of men to be bowled over by such a siren, while I......

But it was hard to say how she was treated. Her brother was just the same as usual, and neither man exactly ignored her, but, in her unreasonable frame of mind, she fancied that she saw in the singer's manner a conceited, world-weary affectedness, a barely veiled lack of interest in her; the off-hand rudeness of the famous, busy man when in the presence of the ordinary. She sat, toying with her food. Ever since T-ray had told her about this new job and ever since her rekindled interest in Emilio Monza himself, Melyssa had looked forward to involving herself in the design work, in the choosing of materials, in the selection of suppliers. She focussed on his project, not on his fame as a celeb, and adjusted her expectations to knowing personally a man for whom many women would have given a great deal just to say they had met him.

Yet – yet who the *hell* did he think he was, treating her with less ceremony than the maid who tidied his hotel room? Melyssa was used to gauging racial slights, but was a long way from realising that her almost adolescent insecurities stemmed largely from her sense of inferiority as a woman; her stunted emotional life sacrificed to her need to succeed socially and in business.

'Ha, ha!' roared T-ray at a joke of the Contessa's. Go on, crawler, thought Melyssa, be her bloody lapdog. She sat, hating her brother for his grovelling, hating Monza for his off-hand arrogance – but most of all she hated herself for that something inside her which responded to Emilio as a man and expected a response in turn, that something which could not keep her eyes from his wrists and the curved grace of his upper arms and the strong legs she could glimpse under the table in their dark trousers, even as he seemed to look through her.

As the asparagus with beurre noisette have way to entrecote of beef bordelaise, all she was conscious of was a sour disappointment and anger.

It was over. Because of parking and the congestion charge T-ray and Melyssa had come to the Dorchester by public transport. They were now in a taxi to Victoria. Melyssa stormed at her brother.

'You damned fool! How could you get me – us – into something like that? The great Monza has picked our little firm to do up his grand theatre for him. God, God! The arrogance of the man! Did you see how he treated me – or rather, how he didn't?' Melyssa was becoming incoherent. 'And that *woman*! Oh, yes, you liked her well enough, crawling up to every word – and to him too! I've never felt so, so left out of things in my life. We've done contracts this last year, and we've met clients together, and I ask you, have I *ever* been so ignored? I notice he asked *you* all the technical questions – in the pauses between your grovelling to the Contessa, that is. Well, I can tell you now, T, I'm not sodding interested. I don't want the job. I wouldn't take the fucking job if I was starving to death. Sorry, but that's final.'

T-ray gaped at her, open-mouthed. With a younger brother's careless regard, he hadn't noticed that she had been seething like a volcano all during the evening. He had put her silence down to a proper girl's shyness in the presence of a titled person and of a great man.

'And that – that bitch, Loredana!' continued Melyssa, making fists of her hands and smiting the taxi-seat on each side of her. 'That appalling cow! Oooh! How you slimed round her like a spaniel. And how she lorded it over you – the rich white aristo and the obsequious darkie! I know one has to be smooth with the clients, but there's a limit. You were mesmerised by the money dripping off her. The worst type of dyed-haired Mediterranean vampire, and you had to lie down while she walked all over you.'

'For God's sake!' hooted T-ray. 'Just simmer down, will you?'

The taxi-driver twisted his head round, pricking up his ears. T-ray dropped his voice to a hiss. 'I was doing no more than being pleasant. And I had to do on my bloody own. You were useless. And worse, you were rude. You know Italians like a bit of demonstrativeness. I think I played it just about right.'

'Oh do you, Mister Clever?' retorted Melyssa. 'Well, it might interest you to know what the siren said to me in the ladies.'

'What do you mean?'

'When I went out to the loo at the end, just before you ordered the taxi, Loredana came with me.'

'Yes, yes. So....?'

'While I was primping up my hair, she sidled up to me and said that we were wasting our time. The restoration of the theatre would probably not come off, and Emilio would, in the end, plump for an Italian design house if it did. He hadn't expected Calypso Designs to be run by blacks.'

'What!'

'You heard. So much for thinking you had it all in the bag.'

'Oh, nonsense,' snorted T-ray. 'You must have misunderstood; her English is pretty weird. What do you think we've been up to all afternoon with the solicitors? I'm sure this contract is as solid as the Bank of England.' Yet even as he spoke, T-ray's brow contracted in worry. Melyssa almost felt guilty at having spoilt his evening.

'Anyhow,' she went on, 'I don't feel happy about the thing. Okay, I accept I was a bit touchy this evening, but I don't like either of them – so I don't want to hear any more. As far as I'm concerned, the job's off. Finished. Over. And,' she added, as he was about to speak, 'if you say one more word I'll scream.'

Brother and sister sat silent in the taxi and then in the train as they went back over the river.

Two days later, as Melyssa sat upstairs at Calypso Designs in jeans, a jumper and with her mop of hair drawn back by a head-band, cross-hatching the shadows around the doorway of a garden-room she was finishing for a client in Putney, and preparing to get the whole thing onto her lap-top as a presentation, there was a jangle at the door. T-ray had popped out in the van, delivering curtains to a lady in Earlsfield, and because Melyssa was busy the showroom downstairs was closed.

'Oh, go away,' muttered Melyssa to herself, jamming down her headband. She gripped her draughtsman's pen between her full red lips, opened her lap-top, checked its battery status and laid her designs next to it.

The bell jingled again.

'Damn it!' snapped Melyssa. She ran downstairs from the design room and was at the showroom door before she could properly see who was there. When she did see, it was too late to retreat.

'Christ!' she gasped and, hating herself for doing so, she tried to tidy her hair with her fingers and pulled her jumper straight.

Through the wide glass she saw Emilio Monza, calm looking and, even in yellow trousers and a loose shirt, managing to lend a spot of glamour to the little street. Behind him was a long, low silver car.

Melyssa opened the glass door. The weak sunlight made her narrow her eyes. Emilio, standing on the pavement while she was on the step, was now her height. His black eyes, searching and shrewd, played about her face. She felt she looked anything but her best – but, she told herself, why should that matter? With the sun behind his upper half and the car framing his lower half, he seemed masterful and, Mel noted angrily, rather amused – tickled, no doubt, at finding himself slumming it with the artisans. Seeing her screwed-up gaze going beyond him, he said,

'Ah, the car. Yes. You are wondering why I'm suddenly mobile. My friend *Il Bimbo*'– and here he named-dropped the nickname of the most fashionable Italian restaurateur in London – 'lends it to me when I'm over.' And as Melyssa continued to gape at him, he added, 'May I come in?'

'Oh, er, of course, I – I'm sorry,' stammered Melyssa, moving out of the doorway. Emilio stepped into the design shop. He was carrying a thin leather brief-case. 'You'd better come up to the studio.' Melyssa felt she had put this ungraciously and she tried to make amends. 'Well, this is a surprise.' She gestured for him to go ahead of her on the stairs.

'Is it?' he answered.

In the studio, which stretched the width and length of the Victorian house, there was an opulent leather sofa – T-ray's favourite sprawling place.

'May I….?' murmured Emilio, sitting and crossing his legs. He set the case against the sofa's arm.

He does look elegant, thought Melyssa. She had no admiration of the scruffy, part-trimmed beard, torn denim look of some of her brother's friends.

'What do you want with me?' she said, horrified immediately by the brusque way she had put it.

'I think it is time I explained why I chose Calypso Designs for my project. I did not go into it fully last time I spoke with you both.'

'I have to say that I am not keen on the job at your tower,' said Melyssa. 'I've told T-ray. What he does is up to him, I'm busy enough right now.'

'Have you thought that you and T-ray are really not at all alike?' said Emilio. 'Can you guess why?'

This was such an unexpected question that Melyssa could think of no response. 'And won't you sit down? This sofa is quite big enough for two.' To Melyssa this remark sounded suggestive – and chauvinistic. She would not have been surprised to see him pat the leather by his side.

'I'm quite happy here, thank you,' she said primly, perching herself on her draughtsman's stool. She wished at once that she had not done this, for her position offered the great tenor a fine view of her long legs. Still, she could hardly move again. She waited for him to continue, but he seemed to hesitate.

'Go on,' she prompted, feeling more in command now she was higher than he was. Again he hesitated.

As she stared at him, there was the sound of a door opening and closing downstairs. Her brother had returned. She called out, 'T, I'm upstairs and we've got a visitor.'

T-ray came up the stairs two at a time and looked into the studio.

'Signor Monza! I might have guessed it was you, seeing the car in the street. Look, those slots are permit only until 6.30. You'll get a ticket if you leave it there much longer. You can drive down and over the main road and find a mobile phone pay meter, or I can lend you our permit to stick on the dashboard. The van is in the alley, so it doesn't need it. The alley isn't big enough for both, unfortunately.'

'I'd better not get a ticket,' smiled Emilio. 'It isn't my car. I'll use your permit, if I may.'

'Toss over the keys and I'll nip down and stick it on the dashboard.'

While T-ray was doing this, Melyssa returned to the unexpected question.

'T-ray and I not alike? Well, no, in some respects we're not, but....'

'I meant that you don't look alike. Skin tone, features, hands, hair. And you haven't thought that interesting?'

Melyssa was about to enquire what on earth Emilio meant by bringing up such an odd topic, when T-ray returned.

'I was telling your sister that I had more news about the project,' said Emilio. 'Not, of course, that she is your sister.'

'*What!*' cried T-ray. 'What do you mean?'

'You are not brother and sister. You are half-brother and half-sister. Did you not know?'

T-ray slumped onto the sofa.

'What on earth are you talking about?'

Melyssa was too stunned to say anything. It was not just the information, if true, that staggered her, but how Emilio Monza could know anything at all about her family.

'I had better explain,' said Emilio, looking disconcerted. 'I really had not meant to shock you both. I would have thought you had known.'

'Known what?' gasped T-ray.

'About your mother.'

'Our mother! Our mother has lived in Bristol all her life. She's married to our father, Abraham Mosengo. He's originally from Ghana.'

'I know that,' replied Emilio. 'But wind the clock back to 1971 – over fifty years ago. In that year Rosa and Frederico D'Andrea were married at Borgo San Martino. In 1973 their son Raffaello was born. Frederico's brother Giovanni was *my* father and in 1983 his wife gave birth to me.'

'But – but you're not called D'Andrea,' interjected T-ray.

'It is my family name,' said Emilio. 'Monza was my choice for a stage name – probably because I like the motor race.' He smiled boyishly.

'Okay. Fine. But how does this link up with our mum?' asked Melyssa.

There was a silence while he wondered how she would take news which, he realised, would be a tremendous shock to her.

'My distant cousin Raffaello was your father, Melyssa.'

He sat, amused by the stupefaction in their faces.

'So I am related,' he went on. 'That is a big part of my interest in Calypso Designs. See?'

'Oh God. God. Yes, I see now. But – but how did your cousin get to know our mother and where? She has not lived outside Bristol.'

'Raffaello was a linguist. He spoke perfect English – as I hope I do now – and he went on a bursary to Bristol University. He met your mother, Yolanda, in 1993. They fell in love and you, *Signorina*, were born in 1995, as you know.'

'How on earth did they meet?'

'Yolanda Cavendish, as she was then, worked at the Blue Riband travel agents. In the days before people booked things on-line you went into the agency to arrange flights. Raffaello met her there.'

'Do....do you mean', asked Melyssa, who felt quite shocked in her astonishment, 'that you have been in touch with our family over the last thirty years? Our mother has never mentioned it.'

'No, of course not,' said Emilio. 'Let me finish this first part of the story. My poor cousin died of leukaemia the same year that you were born, Melyssa. He had been getting ill for a year before then. He and Yolanda never married. They lived as partners in his little flat. She went on earning for both of them; he worked at translations of English into Italian and vice-versa, until his health failed him.'

Melyssa and T-ray looked at each other.

'What a sad story,' said Melyssa. 'I am so sorry about your cousin. Oh, about *my* father. But Mum has never mentioned him. She married our Dad in 1997; the wedding photos are in the sitting-room, but it's the very same year of your cousin's death. I think that sounds a bit strange.'

'Perhaps not,' said Emilio, 'when you consider that she had a tiny child, you, Melyssa, to bring up, still an infant who could not have known her real father. Abraham Mosengo did a very gallant thing. He clearly loved your mother very much.'

'And to think I always thought of him – think of him – as my dad,' said Melyssa, shaking her head.

'He *has* been your father – for twenty-nine years.'

'And I was born in 1998,' murmured T-ray. 'So he really *is* mine.'

'Yes he is. You're twenty-six.' Said Emilio.

'I can see, I suppose, why you wanted to put some biz in the way of your cousin's child,' said T-ray, his brows drawn down. 'Very kind of you, of course. But how did you trace us?'

'It was your mother I traced. It sounds melodramatic, like in a film, but I put a firm of private detectives onto it. Starting from the Blue Riband travel agency to the building society where she works now. She has only had three jobs, all well-documented, all in Bristol. Once I'd got her NI number, the investigators could work through her contributions and where they came from.'

'And finding out about Calypso Designs?'

'Ah. One of my detectives came to see your mother saying that he was from the DWP. He was enquiring where her children were now working, and he said he feared he might have some out-of-date info. Yolanda, your mum, told him about Calypso. The rest was easy.'

'Well, I never,' gasped Melyssa, staring at the smooth talking Italian.

'Now comes the next segment,' smiled Emilio.

'Before we get on to any more revelations,' said Melyssa, getting up from her stool. 'I think I'd like a coffee, or perhaps tea. I'm stunned by all this. How about you, Signor Monza?'

'*Multo gentile,*' smiled Emilio. '*Caffe. Grazie.*'

'T?'

'After all that I'd like something a bit stronger than tea,' grinned her brother. 'Have we any of that brandy left?'

'You could have a dash in your coffee,'

'Good idea. I could do with a hot drink, I guess.'

Melyssa darted about, fetching mugs, boiling a kettle, checking there was milk and sugar and finding a little half-bottle of brandy. Emilio unpacked papers from his briefcase and spread some out beside him.

'You see what I meant about you two not really looking similar. Your hair, Melyssa, is African, so is yours, T-ray, but there is much less brown in your complexion, Melyssa. After all your mother is herself of mixed race. Abraham has given T-ray much darker skin.'

The half-brother and sister gazed at each other. 'I should add that you are both very good-looking,' said Emilio, his eyes dwelling for a moment on Melyssa. 'That is something your second cousin can say, is it not?'

'What are the new revelations?' asked T-ray as they sipped their coffee.

'Borgo San Martino is on the road from Lucca to Montecatini Terme. It is built on a steep hill, as so many Tuscan towns are. Now I'm not the only person you know from Borgo. You've met the Contessa Frosinone, of course. My father had a sister called Gloria and she married Count Alberto Frosinone in 1976. Their son Dominico, another cousin, was born in 1978 and he married Loredana in 2008 when she was twenty.'

'So that's how she fits in,' nodded T-ray. 'Yet if she married as recently as 2008, how come she's a widow?'

'Another very sad thing. Count Alberto died naturally in 2006 aged seventy-three and the title passed to Dominico. So did responsibilities. He was an extensive landowner with many farmers on leased farms, growing what you would expect in Tuscany: vineyards, olive trees, peaches. Loredana hadn't much feeling for all that. She was from Florence and liked the city. She wanted, ideally, to move to Rome. I'm not at all sure she was that upset when Count Dominico lost his life in that aircraft crash in the Alps in 2019. Do you remember that? She was thirty-one then. She's now only thirty-six.'

'Your family life is so dramatic!' put in T-ray. 'It's like something from a lurid novel, or an Netflix six-part drama!'

'There's more drama to come. Borgo San Martino has, at its peak, a wonderful towered *palazzo* with huge spaces inside. It's currently a bit of a ruin but with work it would make a marvellous theatre.'

'*Il Torre del Purgatorio!*' cried Melyssa. 'It is the same one, isn't it?'

Her Black Tower! Could it be that?

She shook her head at the thought. What? Some strange premonition driving her dreams? Nonsense!

Emilio went on, 'In 1960 there had been talk of demolishing the structure. It was the beginning of the time of *Il Miracolo Italiano*, the Italian Miracle: the whole country being modernised post-war. Borgo had no electricity until the late-'fifties. Now pylons were sweeping across Tuscany from Florence to Pisa and Via Reggio, and Borgo's hilltop was the perfect spot. Frederico had fought all modernisation plans. For him, agriculture came first. The land on the hill had belonged to Cinthio D'Andrea, father of Frederico, my father and Gloria, who married Count Frosinone and whose son Dominico married Loredana.'

'And you want to build a theatre? And the Contessa doesn't?'

'She has no say, as yet. My idea is like your government's talk of "levelling up". There are great theatres at which opera is performed in Milan, Turin, Rome, Verona, but not in central Tuscany.'

'It is a lovely idea, I see that,' said Melyssa. 'Quite romantic.'

Her face softened as she spoke. My God, thought Emilio, when she stops being defensive and suspicious and lets her face show her feelings, she is ravishing, charming. For a moment he gazed at her. She looked at him, her dark lashes helping her eyes become aware and interested. Now, you idiot, he said to himself, just you stop these thoughts. What sense is there in having romantic notions about a little decorator from South London? She's made it plain she dislikes you and she has decided she is not interested in the project. And yet, I'll not give up on her. Melyssa seemed to read his thoughts, for her expression changed and she sat more upright on her stool. She felt it was time to say what Loredana had said to her in the Dorchester.

'Look,' she started, 'I'm not agreeing to this project just because I think the idea is a nice one. What has a village in Italy got to do with my life? Besides, your cousin....'

'...cousin by marriage....'

'Loredana said to me in the ladies at the hotel that she didn't think you'd go ahead with the plans once your enthusiasm had cooled and that you certainly wouldn't use a little firm in Battersea run by a couple of blacks.'

'Oh, she couldn't have said that,' interjected T-ray.

'She damn well did. Now I know she doesn't want this – this tower place developed, I understand more why she doesn't want us involved. In any case, surely, Signor Monza, you'd want to entrust the decoration and equipping of such a place to an expert. I mean, we are experts, but our field has been a little more modest that what you are proposing.'

Melyssa stopped, wondering if she was being absurd putting off such a rich client. Normally she would never have confessed that a job was beyond her, but he just *couldn't* take her or her brother seriously as professionals. It nettled her to think he felt an obligation to ask Calypso to do the work because of vague "auld lang syne" familial links.

'I am confident that Calypso will do a fine job,' said Emilio. 'Let us say I am seldom wrong about such things. I have an *instinct*.' In a filmic way he tapped the side of his nose meaningfully – like a *mafioso* arranging a hit. At this thought, Melyssa grinned. Then he spoilt the moment by adding, 'Besides, I always get what I want in the end.'

'You've got details there?' asked T-ray.

'Certainly I have,' said Emilio, reaching down and bringing the contents of the briefcase onto the sofa. 'First of all I have two sketches in water-colour of what the finished theatre will look like. I did them myself. It just shows that singers can do more than sing.' He threw back his head and grinned at Melyssa. He's got a hell of an opinion of himself, she thought. The sketches were good, she had to admit. 'I've also got here a memory-stick with some computer-generated images; they weren't done by me, I admit. Can we use the PC on the desk?'

Shoving the stick into the USB socket, Emilio also spread out a large sheet of architectural drawings. The three of them examined the projections, a clear map of the area and a ground-elevation and floor drawing.

'Looks impressive,' said T-ray.

'The architect who did these is Pietro da Migliorino. He's very well-known in Italy. You can see the scale. It's drawn down to the last detail, *except* interior design, of course.'

'Who will come to hear opera or see plays at your theatre?' asked Melyssa. As had happened before, Melyssa felt that her question sounded graceless. 'I mean,' she went on, 'Borgo is a bit off the beaten track, isn't it? Neither Lucca nor Montecatini are Florence, if you see what I mean. Where will your audience come from?'

'That is a fair question, *Signorina* – and the first my backers asked,' replied Emilio, not seeming put out by Melyssa's lack of enthusiasm. 'Have you heard of Torre del Lago?'

Melyssa shook her head. Another Tower! Italy seemed over-run by them.

'Torre del Lago is where Puccini was born and there is, in the summer, a festival at a big specially-built amphitheatre there. It is even further from Florence than Lucca, yet tens of thousands flock there to hear *"Turandot"* and *"Madame Butterfly"* and *"Tosca"*. I have performed there myself. I was Pinkerton in *"Butterfly"* three years ago. I suppose the very top-rank singers do not often feature there – so I'm unlikely to be on that stage again.'

You would have to say that, wouldn't you? thought Melyssa.

'What you need to know,' went on the great tenor, 'is that my *Gran Teatro Torre del Purgatorio* – a wonderful name, don't you think? – will be Italy's equivalent of Britain's Glyndebourne. You must have heard of that. It's miles from London in Sussex, yet it has great prestige, and attracts an enormous audience.'

'Sounds hip, but why are you so taken with the idea?' asked T-ray.

'I know you two think me vain, egotistical probably, but I'm sure my theatre will redeem me in your eyes.'

'Hey, I don't think that,' said T-ray.

'I do,' retorted Melyssa.

' Look, this is no ordinary theatre. Where do you think I come from? A peasant family, as we would say in Italy – not rich, the previous generation not well-educated. My father left school at twelve. A relative paid for part of my musical studies, but only after I had a break and performed. The state gave me a bursary too, as they had done for Raffaello, but again only after I had begun to have luck. Without luck, nothing. Do you think I'd be staying at the Dorchester if not for luck?'

'But you have your talent, surely? And you must have worked hard,' said T-ray.

'I do have talent. It would be false modesty of me not to admit it. And of course I have worked hard on practice, on small engagements, on exhausting tours, on recording sessions. Let me let you that learning the part of Siegfried in Wagner is not an easy way of making a living.'

'But you think chance is the most important element?' asked Melyssa.

'Oh yes. Many, many people have sublime talent and work hard, but without that lucky break, that lucky engagement, they get nowhere.'

'Hm, I've got a few friends who want to make it in film and on the stage and are still *baristas* in Starbuck's after busting their guts to get discovered, and *not* being discovered,' grinned T-ray.

'I want to lessen the dependence on luck for as many as I can. I have money now that I do not know what to do with. An endowment scheme for poor singers, a school and a place to perform as a showcase for them, with my influence behind it, the support of other top names; many boys and girls might follow the path which I got onto by chance.'

Emilio thrust the remaining documents towards them. T-ray and Melyssa studied them intently. There was a design for the approach up from the town, for the music school and its accommodation and rehearsal facilities, the designs for dormitory rooms, dining areas and, the centre-piece, the sinuous elevations which Pietro da Migliorino had prepared for the theatre itself – a sweeping façade enwrapping the base of the existing medieval tower.

It did look a splendid scheme, Melyssa had to admit. That element of helping others, young gifted people from ordinary backgrounds, made all the difference. It was not, as she had first thought it, a spoilt, rich celeb's self-glorying toy.

She saw at once that it would be a multi-million dollar investment and would become a talking-point beyond Italian shores. She realised it would be insane not to want to become part of it. Already her trained mind was ruminating colours, materials and lighting.

'Ah, I see you *are* interested, after all, *Signorina*,' murmured Emilio.

Melyssa turned her face to him. Their eyes met.

'I want to be part of this contract, yes,' admitted Melyssa.

'And you said earlier….' Began T-ray.

'I know, but now I know more…..'

'But you already *have* the contract,' laughed Emilio.

'Yes, but the Contessa, your cousin, did say yesterday that she thought it was touch and go,' put in Melyssa, recalling Loredana's manner at the hotel,

'It is I who make contracts,' snapped Emilio, his brow contracting.

I wish I knew what was between those two, and what the Contessa's real feelings were, thought Melyssa. She noted the lines of experience round his eyes. She felt him appraising her skin, her lips, her body. It might have been imagination, but she fancied that, taking the designs from her hand, he had stroked the skin of her arm. As she internalised these impressions, she told herself not to be so stupid. He doesn't know you. You've only just met. He's probably the Contessa's lover. He's ten years older than you. He's famous and rich – and you're not. You're in a bad way emotionally. Twenty-nine and no one cares about you. He isn't likely to. You're hotting up and making something out of nothing. Don't tell yourself that your instinct isn't wrong. Grow up, woman.

'So that's it then for the moment?' asked T-ray. 'I ask because we have a couple of commitments to sort out.'

'Yes, I know. Have you managed to do what we discussed yesterday?' asked Emilio, making for the door.

'Oh yes. I've wound up the Holman's biz and got Joe onto getting their pelmets up.'

'What are you saying?' asked Melyssa. 'Why are we rushing the Holman's job? They're good clients.'

'Oh, didn't Signor Monza explain that before I arrived? We leave, Sis, for Pisa on Thursday.'

'Oh, you creep! You bastard! How can you *do* this to me?' wailed Melyssa into her phone.

Thursday, cool and drizzly, had arrived, and the "Calypso Designs" duo were flying out to Pisa from Gatwick late morning. T-ray had rung her very early with a croaking voice to say that he had a fever and a cough and, testing himself, had managed to pick up Covid.

'I know it's crap for you, of course, but I – I just really feel I can't go on my own. I need your moral support on this job.'

'For heaven's sake, Mel, you're not going to Yemen or a Siberian gulag. You're bloody lucky to be getting away from this weather. Just go and be grateful. You'll be met at Pisa. I'll join you as soon as poss. I'll be able to get a flight okay. It'll be five or six days max. Just keep me in the loop. Text or ring. You'd better get going, Sis. Give my best to the guys out there.' He rang off, coughing.

Melyssa dropped the phone among her bedclothes, having checked it again for the time. 6.45. Horrendous. But then she had to be at Gatwick a couple of hours before the flight. Time to get up.

It was ridiculous – this feeling of being afraid to set off alone. For God's sake, she told herself, you're twenty-nine, and you're going to do the job of a lifetime for a household name, who is a relative, in sunny Italy, and you whinge like a brat going to school for the first time. Professional, successful designer, or whining, pathetic cow? Choose.

Melyssa had not been idle since the Dorchester meeting at the beginning of the week. She had skimmed her copies of "*Abode 2*" and other magazines to get suppliers to look up, had taken three trips to the Design Centre at Chelsea Harbour, gradually amassing ideas on the materials, furniture and lighting she would import into Italy from the UK, and had spent hours on-line with the design houses in Florence with whom "Calypso Designs" were going to cooperate. Her homework had been paying off – and now this blow.

Since she had been shown the scale of the project, Melyssa had not been able to sleep well. The prospect of having such a big say in the décor, fittings and layout of a complex of buildings the size of a village was daunting. She found herself leaping off her pillow at odd hours during the night and jamming ideas and calculations onto the lap-top by her bedside. Sometimes, in dreams, Emilio would stand frowning at her. Sometimes Loredana, Contessa di Frosinone, featured. Once they were mixed up in dreams about the black tower, clinging together laughing at her while she photographed the tower inside and out. At these times, they cackled in Italian, which Melyssa did not understand. Upon wakening, she had to remind herself that they all spoke English – the *'lingua franca'* of the EU, even though, absurdly, the UK was no longer part of it all since the disaster of Brexit.

Toughen up, woman. What has to be done, will be done. You can cope. Yet it had been comforting that T-ray and she were going out to the site together. Now this awful news. Melyssa felt lonely and inadequate. She had never tackled a job on her own before. She had never gone abroad on her own. Emilio Monza would be there, but she had mixed feelings about being alone with him. She was sure that he found her alluring – and that was both intriguing and worrisome. In his presence she managed to be a gawky, inexperienced schoolkid, and, like one of those, she withdrew into graceless clumsy moods.

As these reflections chased themselves across her mind while she dressed and packed, she had a picture of Rebecca. Would she behave as Melyssa was doing? Rebecca, about to get sausages from the Co-op for Wotsisname? For Dennis. That's it. Cooking sausages for Dennis' supper day after day. Would Rebecca fail to seize the chance I've got? Look how much further I've come than Rebecca. If I don't pull myself together, I've no right to feel superior to Rebecca, and I might just as well have stayed in Bristol living at home. Consultant Designer, indeed! What am I really? And what *have* I got? A little shop in Battersea selling knick-knacks. And I behave to Rebecca, and to Mum, as if I'm the successor to Terence

Conran, or the new Kelly Hoppen. If it hadn't been for Emilio and his detective work, I'd be selling cushions to punters in Clapham for the rest of my working life.

These bitter thoughts chased each other through her head while Melyssa got up. She stared into the bathroom mirror. She looked peaky; there were dark smudges under her eyes and she had a shadow of a headache coming on. She alternated between hoping that she too had picked up T-ray's Covid and praying that she hadn't. Her test was negative.

Just before T-ray's early phone call she had had an odd dream. In this one Loredana had not appeared, but she had heard a woman's voice crying: Melyssa, watch your step. The treads are slimy. The voice seemed to be her own. Then she was falling inside the Black Tower. Above was a circle of light; beneath her a sloping stage. Dim faces looked up at her. Falling with her, but also walking at normal pace was Emilio Monza. His hair was wet and he wore a cloak. His face was very close to hers in the dark. His eyes burned. With a shock she noticed he wore nothing beneath the airy folds of the cloak. She was so excited by this that she was unprepared for the impact as the floor of the tower met her. Something she had heard about relaxing limbs to survive a fall darted into her mind, but her hands were reaching for Emilio's arms, her legs were round his body, so when the impact came at the bottom of the black tower it was in an explosion of red.

Melyssa brushed her teeth and saw through the venetian blind the damp London street. She shook the grisly cobwebs from her brain.

Gatwick. EasyJet. 1.30 flight. Taxi to Victoria. Gatwick Express. No ASLEF strikes today, thank God. Melyssa checked her tickets, passport and Euros, booked an Uber, hoisted her little suitcase, locked up and left.

Too queasy at home to eat more than a couple of biscuits with her tea, she found she could manage her in-flight snack, and, in spite of the noise round her, fell into a doze until the Captain's voice awakened her,

'….and to your left the Leaning Tower of Pisa as we approach Galileo Galilei.'

Melyssa clutched the sides of her seat. No turning back now.

'Cara Signorina!'

Melyssa knew the cry of greeting was aimed at her. With her dark glasses in their wallet in her suitcase, she had stumbled out of the 'plane into blinding Pisan sunshine and a bodily slap of 24C heat. In London it had been 13C. While she waited for her case to appear on the carousel, she heard again the loud, imperious call from the glass-panelled doors at the end of the arrivals area.

'Signorina Mosengo! Venga qui, per favore! Qui!'

Contessa Frosinone, Emilio's cousin, stood framed in the metal doorway. The other waving and waiting Italians stood away from her. She tapped a customs officer on the arm, favouring him with a dazzling smile. He bowed, then made his way over to where Melyssa stood, hoping that her case would soon appear. It did a moment later, and he took it up.

'You come out. No worry, *Signorina*. The Contessa she wait for you.'

Melyssa began to say something in her faltering Italian, gave up, and allowed herself to be led towards the exit door. The English contingent were left behind. I expect they wonder who I am, thought Melyssa. Loredana seized her arm and gave her a brief, hard, pecking kiss.

'So nice to see you again,' she murmured.

Melyssa was taken through the taxi-drivers and a jabbering crowd to the Contessa's car. A blue-jawed, glossy young man darted forward. A rear door was opened, and the women were ushered into the back. Loredana beamed on all around her.

'Cara Signorina, I 'ope you have had the good journey, but it is vairy short, *si?'*

Melyssa would have spoken but she felt robbed of words. It wasn't just that she spoke little Italian, but she couldn't quite believe in the sincerity of the Contessa. Somehow, although he hadn't said he was going to, she had expected Emilio to have met her. She had instinctively disliked Loredana in London, and believed it to be mutual, but here, on home ground, Melyssa had to take in how magnificently assured and how rich the Contessa seemed to be. The old cliché: "You can't be too rich or too thin" drifted into her mind as Loredana uncrossed her legs, leaned forward and, with a red-taloned finger, pressed a button on the console between the backs of the two front seats.

'Drink?' she asked, taking out a bottle of Campari soda and a tin of 7-Up. The tin she tossed over the seat-back to the young driver.

'Er....' started Melyssa, who didn't want anything.

'Campari, *cara*?'

'Thank you. Yes. I mean, *si*.'

'My husband like to have cold drinks in the car when it is 'ot. So I have them too, even after he is – is....*morto*.'

'Dead,' Melyssa interposed, as the Contessa seemed to be having difficulty with the right word. 'I am so sorry.'

'*Grazie.* You like my car? It is a Bentley. British.'

'Yes, very much. I've never been in a Bentley. Or a Rolls.'

After this crass comment, which she wished she hadn't made, Melyssa could think of nothing else to say. They whirled along past innumerable trees, each trunk painted with a white band. Progress was silent, except for the thump of heavy tyres on the pitted tarmac.

Loredana and the driver began to speak in Italian, and each laughed once or twice. Melyssa caught the young man's eyes in his rear-view mirror. Inside, she burned with mortification to think that they might be discussing her. Why did T-ray have to get Covid? How different it would have been if his effervescent, irrepressible personality were in the car with them.

After their drinks were finished and Loredana had lit a sweet-scented cigarette, Melyssa became aware that the sea was still visible on the left.

She had pored over maps of the area before she had left and was sure that Lucca lay inland towards Florence. She realised now that they were heading north and a sense of alarm began to creep over her. Back came the Contessa's odd, hostile words to her in the ladies' room at the Dorchester. Was that what she and the young chauffeur had been discussing? The fact that she would, in some way, never see Borgo and never end up doing the Black Tower job at all? She nerved herself to ask a direct question.

'Aren't we going to Borgo?'

'No. We go to Monte Bulciano. Our 'ouse. It is on the coast above Via Reggio. It is the development which will be at Borgo. We live at sea. You meet Emil there later.'

A huge and ridiculous flood of relief poured over Melyssa. What a dramatising fool you are! Who the hell's going to kidnap *you*? Her fears allayed, Melyssa turned her thoughts to what Loredana had just told her. She wondered whether or not the Contessa's English was up to explaining what she meant by the phrase "our house", but before she could think out a carefully worded question to find out if Loredana lived with Emilio, the car turned into a stone gateway. Loredana ground out the last of what had been her sixth cigarette and wriggled her short skirt down her thighs. Melyssa gazed from the window. At the end of a steep, orange-planted drive was an attractive warm-yellow villa.

'You come in. Gabriello will see to your bag,' said Loredana, and, getting out elegantly, she swayed up the steps ahead of Melyssa on her high heels. Beneath green and white awnings a dapper man in a cream jacket waited. 'Sidney,' called the Contessa, 'this is *Signorina* Mosengo, the London decorator. *Signorina*, this is Sidney, my cousin's secretary.'

'Sidney Gill, Signor Monza's secretary *and* manager *and*... friend,' said a high, soft, carefully modulated American voice, pausing for a fraction before the last word.

Squinting into the setting sunlight, Melyssa peered into the shadows with screwed-up face and shook the American's hand. Thank God someone else speaks English round here, she thought.

'You 'ungry?' asked the Contessa. '*Buono*,' she continued, without waiting for Melyssa to reply. 'Me, I am ravished.'

Sidney Gill smiled unkindly after Loredana as she glided into an inner salon.

'You'll only be ravished if you pay for it, sweetie,' he murmured.

Melyssa, catching the smile and the comment, realised that Loredana was not admired by the smooth, soft-voiced American. 'I guess I'm keeping you from unpacking before dinner,' he said to her. 'I'm sure you didn't touch that horrible stuff they give you on the flight. We're looking forward to giving you a proper Tuscan dinner, Miss Mosengo. It's a little early, so plenty of time for you to freshen up in your room. Gabriel will show you where you will be staying.'

But where, thought Melyssa, was Emilio? The Bentley had left Galileo Galilei not long after 4.00. It was now 6.15. He must be planning to join us for the meal.

After she had unpacked in her room – a pleasant, large space with a view of the Carrara mountains and an en-suite bathroom – Melyssa, in the only dress she had brought with her, came down to the dining-salon overlooking the sea. She stared in dismay at the heaps of salad, fruit and cheeses. An small elderly woman helped her to a plate of prosciutto and melon. Melyssa ate with all the appetite she could. She was then given a large square of *lasanga verde*. She slowed down, taking small forkfuls. The wispy little woman went back to the kitchen.

'*Dio mio!*' cried Loredana, stubbing out her cigarette in the glass ashtray by her arm, 'anyone would think the *Americano* 'as not eat since last week! Look at him.'

Sidney smiled at Melyssa.

'I guess you work up an appetite going through the papers and correspondence that Emilio's project is generating.'

'I'm sure you do,' replied Melyssa.

'Ada!' called Sidney. '*Encora lasagna, per favore.*'

Ada came in with a large dish, and gave Melyssa another slab before serving Sidney.

'Oh, er, no. *Basta, grazie,*' Melyssa protested, but it was too late.

'You. You do nothing but eat,' said Loredana unpleasantly to Sidney.

'This woman,' said Sidney, turning ostentatiously towards Melyssa, 'makes the mistake of thinking that behaving like a bad-tempered, spoilt brat is a sign of good breeding. But,' he went on, punctuating his words with large bites of lasagna, 'if you look at the hands, Miss Mosengo, you will see that they are greedy, grasping, stubby hands – like a chimp's. A monkey's!' he suddenly cried, spitting out lasagna as he did so, 'Your hands, by contrast, Miss Mosengo, show that you are an artist.'

'You dare to….?' spluttered the Contessa, dropping her fork with a clatter.

'Er….' began Melyssa.

'She,' said Sidney Gill, gesturing with his knife, 'married into money. The late Count had plenty all right, although how much is left is anyone's guess the rate she's spending it since he died. But she came out of the hills. Without her money and the title he gave her she would be nothing.'

Loredana rose from her chair. Considering how severely she had been insulted and provoked, she maintained a calm dignity. But it was a dreadful calm, ominous and bitter.

'Your rudeness gets worse and worse,' was all she said.

'Don't lecture me on manners, and how I eat, my dear Contessa, if you don't want a lesson in rudeness in return,' replied Sidney.

Melyssa, more embarrassed than she could say, laid down her knife and fork. She too stood up.

'I really think I might go…..' she muttered.

'Sit down, please, Miss Mosengo. Nothing new,' drawled Sidney. 'Come on, Loredana, sit, can't you? You are spoiling Miss Mosengo's first meal in Italy. Ada! Ada!'

Ada came out again, took the lasagna plates away and handed out new ones. From her trolley she took roast meat and helped Melyssa to a large heap of it. Sidney gave her salad.

'That's right,' snarled Loredana, 'make a fuss over the little decorator.' To Melyssa she said, 'You and I know what you are doing here. So let's have no games. My cousin says he has a family obligation to you and your brother. We shall see. There is no point in Mister Sidney Gill getting too friendly with you. I don' think you are going to be here long.'

'Jumping Jehosaphat, you are the limit,' said Sidney, glaring at the Contessa. 'Well, Ada's gone a lot of trouble with this meal, so I think we should pay her the compliment of enjoying it. There's a nice dessert coming, Miss Mosengo. Tuscan speciality.'

The rest of the ghastly meal was spent in silence. Melyssa, not feeling in the least hungry, forced herself to eat as much as she could. All the time she wondered where Emilio was. Outside it was now dark.

Loredana rose.

'I'm going to speak to Ada. Then I'm going to bed.'

'Not staying to help our guest feel at home? Well, I guess I'm up for that. Let's have coffee on the terrace, Miss Mosengo. It's still warm enough. She,' he said, pointing at the Contessa, 'is not fit company for anyone but the pigs she used to keep.'

He marched out, his thin shoulders straight.

Loredana – who seemed restored to humour by Sidney's anger – gave Melyssa a conspiratorial smile.

'I am certain you 'ave great fun on the terrace,' she sneered. 'I see you later, *caro* – maybe,' she added sweetly.

Melyssa awoke in her bedroom as the light rose over the mountains. Her first thought was of her work in the studio in Battersea. Then she remembered where she was and sighed. The evening of her arrival had been a nightmare. Sidney, over coffee, had tried to bring her out and had encouraged her to talk about herself and her ideas for the project, but she sensed that he had found it hard going. And all the time she wondered where Emilio was. What a report to make to T-ray! She decided not to contact him until part of another day had passed. Surely today couldn't be as frightful as yesterday?

At breakfast, which she and Sidney had on their own because Loredana took hers in her bedroom, Melyssa felt that she must get out of the house and away from its warring inhabitants. The dark blue sea and bright umbrellas of Monte Bulciano seemed infinitely attractive. She mentioned her intention to the silent Sidney. He seemed a lot less effervescent than he had done at dinner.

'Oh, yeah. Why not? Nothing on here yet.'

'When do you think Signor Monza is going to be here?'

Sidney avoided answering and said,

'I hope you didn't find the Contessa too disturbing last might.'

'Well, I must say I hadn't thought that…'

'…..that she hated you? Of course she hates you. Emil has spoken to me about you. You are – if you don't mind my saying so – very attractive, and that woman is no fool.'

'What do you mean? Do you mean to say that….?'

'Yes. Emil is showing a lot of interest in you, Miss Mosengo, and it's not just because of the Black Tower project, and his dear so-called cousin doesn't like it one bit. Up to now *she* has tried to be the focus of interest. She's racially prejudiced too, like a lot of Italians. I heard all about you from her, and I expected the black mammy from "Gone with the Wind". So absurd; you're more Meghan Markle than African Queen.'

'You mean not *too* black,' retorted Melyssa. 'Why not come out and say it? My brother's blacker,' she added, as the new fact of their different parentage occurred to her again.

'Makes no odds with me. With the so-called cousin, it's different.'

Melyssa gazed at Sidney with her clear brown eyes. She felt angry that Emilio had left this welcome committee for her: the waspish secretary and the jealous, prejudiced cousin.

'Why do you keep calling her Emilio's "so-called cousin"?' she asked.

'Loredana married Emilio's aunt's son. They are not blood relations.'

Melyssa wondered if that was, after all, good news, if Emilio and the Contessa had been, or were about to be, lovers.

'Where is he?' she asked directly.

'Emilio? Why, I guess he's on the *Buona Fortuna*, his yacht, down in the marina.' Sidney gestured down to the boats at anchor, half a mile down the hill. 'He was giving a party to the leaders of the Commune of Borgo and some hotel owners and businessmen of Monte Bulciano – whipping up support for the theatre, you know. I organised it all for him. Hey, I guess I'm sorry,' he added with a grin, 'but, important as your arrival was, they just happened to clash. I daresay it went on late and he spent the night on the boat. He'll materialise soon.'

Melyssa pushed back her chair.

'I'll be back later,' she said, and, leaving the American at the table, went up to her room and slipped her swimming costume on under her light dress. A few minutes later, she was swinging along heading for the beach.

As she came out onto the coastal road and saw the boats at anchor in the marina, it occurred to her that she would like to see Emilio's yacht. She might, after all, catch a glimpse of him. She turned her footsteps to the beginning of the wooden gangplanks. The sun was getting hotter and higher and Melyssa remembered that her sunglasses were still at the bottom of her suitcase. She had to screw up her eyes as she tried to make out which of the moored vessels was the *Buona Fortuna* in the little harbour. Failing to spot Emilio's boat, she went into a glass-fronted booth in which an official-looking man sat at a desk.

'*Scusi*,' said Melyssa. 'Which of these boats is the *Buona Fortuna*?'

'*La*,' replied the man, gesturing to a lovely white ship outside the marina.

Instantly she realised that it would be Emilio's yacht. A little way out, at anchor, not moored to the gang-planks at all, was a large, stream-lined double-tiered craft like a small ocean liner. She had expected something on the lines of the pleasure boats she had seen on the Thames.

'*Si, si. E la Buona Fortuna,*' nodded the official.

Melyssa thanked him and walked out down the slope to the hot sand. The yacht looked so close. As she stood peering at it, she felt again the embarrassments she had been put through at the hands of her acquaintances at the house. On a foreign shore, without her sunglasses, in limbo between the large villa and the large yacht of her host – a host who had not come to meet her at the airport – Melyssa's courage and obstinacy born of coping with racial prejudice, real and imagined, rose up inside her. Squinting out across the wavelets, she framed the intention to do the best job that had ever been done on a building, and to show them all! She suddenly felt happy again – confident and capable. Was she not a professional?

The heat grew more intense. Melyssa walked down the beach to the water's edge. She squatted and put her hand in the sea. It was warm but also refreshing. She had a strong desire to swim in it and, turning round to the beach huts and umbrellas which lined the sand, she moved along until she spotted the dressing-rooms and fumbled in her bag for her Euros. She knew that in Italy one had to undress under cover. A woman rose from a chair outside the building, took two Euros, gave her the key to cubicle 47, and smiled and cackled.

Back on the beach, feeling conspicuous as the only black girl there, she ran down the hot sand to the water and plunged in.

'Wonderful!' she gasped. She struck out towards the yacht.

Afterwards, she could not remember the moment when it had seemed a good idea to surprise Emilio by swimming out to his boat. Melyssa had wanted to prove something, she supposed. If he hadn't come to greet her, she would bloody well go to him. She had imagined him calling over the side with a delighted smile, impressed by her prowess as a swimmer and by her amusingly unconventional way of making her arrival known.

The water rushing in her ears, she turned to look back. The beach seemed a long way off. The white yacht seemed no nearer. The water did not feel as warm as it had felt at the sea's edge. She swum on.

Ten minutes later, without warning, her left leg began to cramp. Treading water, each move an agony, she peered shoreward again. The umbrellas were very far off now. Rearing up behind them were the marble peaks of the Carrara mountains. The curve of the coastline went off as far as she could see. Emilio's yacht no longer seemed very near. She struggled on towards it. It was borne upon her mind that she was in deep water and in danger. After another ten minutes, she realised that she was exhausted.

'It looked so close,' she found herself repeating rhythmically.

Using only her right leg, she swam on towards the yacht, each breath now coming with difficulty. Struggling automatically, for she was on the verge of blacking out, she was aware of a dark shadow on the sea. She had, at last, arrived under the stern of *La Buona Fortuna*. She reached out to grasp at a rope which was hanging over the side and she clung to it, gasping and fighting back the waves of darkness. She thought she heard her voice crying out for help. A head appeared above her. She did not know how she did it as, trembling with strain and with a searing pain in her left thigh, she managed to reach up to outstretched arms. She was pulled over the rail onto the deck. There she knelt, retching and coughing until, with a violent shiver, her exhaustion and nausea overcame her and she fainted.

When she came to, she was out of the light. Her eyes opened on the texture of a white pillow. Over her was a shadow. She looked up, startled, trying to collect her senses. Emilio Monza stood by the bed.

'What? Where….? Where am I?'

'So you are better,' said Emilio. His voice sounded unsympathetic, but as she peered up at him, Melyssa could see that his eyes were soft.

'I'm sorry. I – I think I fainted. I shouldn't have swum so soon after breakfast, I suppose….' Her voice tailed off.

'You did a silly thing setting out to swim beyond the shoreline near the marina. Anyone round here will tell you that the beach shelves away quickly and that the current off-shore can be cold. Didn't you see the notices?'

'Oh, no. I – I probably couldn't read them, anyway. I just thought I'd…..'

'A very silly thing to do', interrupted Emilio. 'Irrational.'

Again the irritation in his voice belied the lines of worry in the lines round his eyes.

'Oh, please don't be angry with me. I just….' began Melyssa. She stopped in horror. She had slipped her hand under the sheet and made the discovery that she was naked.

'Oh, yes. You are,' said Emilio, smiling for the first time. 'I could hardly put you in my bed in your wet swimming costume.'

'Did you….?' gasped Melyssa.

'Did I undress you? I came up on deck when Pietro called me. I saw you lying in a pool of water in the sun. The two of us carried you down to my cabin, I took off your costume, dried you and put you to bed. You whimpered once like a child,' added Emilio – again with a smile – 'but,' he continued, seeking her eyes frankly, 'it was not a task that I disliked. You are every inch a beautiful woman. There is not a blemish on your body.'

'Oh!' gasped Melyssa, more horrified than she could express, and more embarrassed than she had ever been, 'Oh! How can you stand and say such things to me? I don't believe that you…. you speak as though you enjoyed….'

'I did,' interposed Emilio. 'I did enjoy handling your naked body. Why not?'

'But who else? I mean, that name you mentioned….'

'He's the yacht's engineer. His quarters are below deck. He won't disturb us. The rest of the crew are in the town or seeing family.'

'But - but the others? Your secretary, Mr Gill, told me that you had a big party of guests aboard.'

As she said this, Melyssa became aware of how much worse it might have been if a large party of local notables had seen her arrival on the yacht. She who was due to design the building interior to which they were going to donate money and support. What a complete fool she would have looked!

Emilio gazed at her, still with a smile difficult to interpret.

'Ah, them. Well….'

'There are no guests from the town on board *now*, are there?' she quavered. 'The crew has gone, and guests…'

'There never *were* any guests, *Signorina*. I own up to it that I instructed Sidney to tell you I was engaged with them when you arrived.'

Melyssa stared at him.

'But why?'

For a moment he looked nonplussed, then his face cleared and he sought her eyes again.

'I have been deeply disturbed since I met you, if want the truth,' he said simply. 'I have thought of little but you and your coming out here for the whole week. I realised that I could not come to the *aeroporto*, to Pisa. I did not know what it would be like seeing your face again. I have been haunted by it in dreams. I suppose I didn't want to be disappointed by reality.'

'And instead of greeting me at Pisa, you find me half-drowned clambering into your yacht. That's a reality even worse. So you must be very disappointed.' She stopped, feeling that it sounded as though she were fishing for compliments.

'As I said a minute ago, I am not at all disappointed,' said Emilio. 'I am disappointed in nothing about you, *cara Signorina.*' He reached out and pulled gently at the sheet which she was clutching round her nudity. 'As I dried you, I was enraptured.'

'Stop it!' she cried, edging backwards on the bed. The quick movement dislodged the sheet and part of it fell away revealing her breasts. She put up a hand to cover her nipples, but Emilio leaned over, took her hand and gently pulled it away. His eyes rested on her naked torso. Now that he was close to the bed, Melyssa could see into his part open shirt the dark hairs on his chest and arms. She catalogued the fact, in spite of her own wonderment at being in this position, that he was not too hairy. She had never admired very hirsute men. His dark little curls were somehow boyish and it made him more desirable, she was amazed to note. What on earth am I doing? How did this happen? Melyssa felt unexpected arousal. She was conscious of the scent of sandalwood on him. He knelt by the bed's edge and, before she could stop him, pulled the sheet fully down and away from her with one hand while seizing her wrist with the other.

'Please let go!' gasped Melyssa. Into her mind came rushing all the advice she had ever had about what to do when a man molested you. She had been to several "Me too" get-togethers and felt that she was equal to any situation. Yet none of the words of experience had covered this particular situation: naked in a celebrity's berth on a yacht moored offshore.

'Please let go of me,' she said again, struggling into a sitting position, almost forgetful of her nakedness in her outrage.

'You came here to find me, I presume,' replied Emilio. 'You sneaked aboard in the morning. You nearly drowned. I tended you and put you into my own bed – *mio letto, Signorina* – and you have treated me as an enemy, an abuser. I didn't come over to the villa and get myself into *your* bed!'

He stood, pulling her up with him. The sheet fell away from her.

'Oooh,' she gasped, grabbing too late at the material.

'From the beginning you have shown me a cold side of your nature. Me, I took you in to work with me in the greatest desire of my heart. You are my uncle's grand-daughter, and your half-brother and I have shown each other warmth and friendliness. You, on the other hand, have been off-hand, disdainful, distant, ungrateful. And then you suddenly come out here after me. No, no, the playing of games is over.'

He took her hand and placed it on the clasp of his white shorts. She had not taken in how scantily he was glad: an open shirt and shorts. He placed her hand on his thigh. Her throat contracted in excitement at the touch of his bare leg. His fingers ran over her breasts and he kissed her neck and her ears. She found her hand pulling at the shorts' clasp, and then seeking the bulge just below. She was aware of his gasp as she did so. Her senses flared with arousal as he slid his fingers between her taut buttocks and lifted her upwards for a kiss. Her legs enwrapped his thighs. He brought his lips to hers, gently at first, then his tongue sought her mouth. He pushed her back onto the bed and swung himself next to her, his fingers locked round her hardening groin. A fire swept through her as her firmed nipples were pushed into his chest. He lifted himself onto her, his hand at the waistband of the shorts.

Then, before he could pull them down, some remnant of awareness of what he was doing to her shot into Melyssa's mind. She was horrified to think how far her own quickly aroused passions had led her. Unprotected, she had been about to make love with a man about whom she knew nothing, whom she had known for barely a week. She marvelled that only yesterday she had been in her little room in London. With this mundane consideration, she twisted in his arms, dragging her face back from his lips and pulling his hands away from her body..

'No, *please*, Signor Monza. I won't let you....'

She dug her fingers into his hair and wrenched his head back. 'You can't do as you like with me! I've said I won't let you. If you go on it will be rape – rape! I don't care who you are, you shan't go on with this!'

She squirmed beneath him. Anger had replaced lust. Unasked, he was going to take her, unprotected, as a possession, and she would not stand for it.

'Ah, ah!' he gasped, as her struggles prevented his entrance of her. She slipped off the bed and stood by the cabin door. He leapt up and was in front of her. She pushed him away, and he stood, facing her, an expression hard to read on his face.

'I've told you I can't let you do it,' said Melyssa firmly. 'You won't do it – *we* won't do it – not like this.'

She watched him lift his arm slowly. She noted the dark curls in his arm-pit and the cords of his muscles; saw with one glance the tanned body which she still found alluring. She saw his arm descend. Melyssa, fearing that he was going to strike her, had sunk to the floor, covering her head with her hands. She heard his voice, amused now and cool,

'Come on, *Signorina*. Do you think I would hit a woman? My arm had cramp in it.'

He turned and left the cabin.

Melyssa tottered to her feet, flung open the cabin door and went to the companionway steps. She was about to climb them when she realised she could hardly swim ashore naked at Monte Bulciano, even had she the strength to make it.

She drew back into the cabin and pushed the door shut. There was no sound aboard the yacht. An onrush of mixed emotions: anger, outrage, frustrated sexual desire, regret, embarrassment and fear swept over her.

'Oh God! God!' cried Melyssa as she sank back on the berth.

The door opened again. Twenty minutes had passed, though to Melyssa it had seemed far longer. She had wrapped herself in the sheet and was sitting shakily on the side of the bed. Emilio stood before her, dressed now in slacks and with shirt buttoned. He had clothing over his arm.

'There,' he said. 'Put these on. The trousers may be a little long, but I'm sure they will suit you.'

He placed some garments of his own on the bed.

'I will leave you to sort yourself out. When you are ready, come up on deck and have some coffee. I am about to go ashore and up to the house for lunch. We'll go together.'

His tone was kindly, concerned and not at all angry. Melyssa could hardly believe that this Emilio was the same man he had been a short time before. He had had time to think and, after letting his arousal subside and now feeling calmer, he had seen that Melyssa was to be admired for her objections to casual sex. How unlike a lot of women he knew.

She felt that she too was hardly the same person who had set out from the beach. Was it wise to have stopped him making love to me? I wanted his love, as much as he wanted to give it. He is the most attractive man I have met. But I won't be taken for granted. And yet – oh, what a muddle it all is!

They had coffee in mugs. By her side Melyssa found a plate of nice-looking biscuits.

'You sit quietly, *Signorina*,' said Emilio. 'Take a *biscotto* with your coffee. They are a *specialita*, made of almonds. Look, I have here your swimming-costume in a plastic bag. Not dry yet, of course. The motorboat is ready when you want to go ashore.'

'Thank you,' mumbled Melyssa.

They went down the short ladder to the motorboat. Emilio perched on one of the two chairs at the front and started the engine.

'Won't you come and sit with me and see the bay as we turn to go in?' he asked.

'Yes. I – I'd like to.' Strangely, she felt that she could join him at the controls. She turned to watch the streamlined yacht as they chugged into the marina. What had happened back there still astonished her. And she was still part-regretting what had not happened.

They both spoke at once,

'I hope that you....'

'I'm sorry if I.....'

'I didn't want you to think.....'

'*Ma, non importa, Signorina.*'

Emilio shrugged his shoulders and concentrated on bringing the motor-boat in past the harbour wall to its mooring-place among the catwalks.

'Won't you call me Melyssa?' said Melyssa timidly.

'*Si.* If you address me as Emilio. I think, after what has happened, we could permit that,' he added, smiling.

She watched him as he steered in. Beneath the shirt and trousers she still saw – and knew she would see forever – his dark-haired body, his long thighs, his olive chest. A vestige of her unfulfilled passion made her lips part for an instant. Her eyes sought the seductive creases of his slacks as he perched next to her. What is going to happen now? she asked herself. Can I stay on and work normally with him after what has gone between us? And then she reflected: what *did* go on between us? We kissed, he was a little rough when excited, but he desired me – and what's wrong with that? I desire him. Yes, Melyssa told herself truthfully, I want to feel again that fire when he kisses me, when he strokes my body.

Melyssa felt she needed a long time alone to come to grips with her questions, her doubts and needs. What she did realise is that her swim out to the *Buona Fortuna,* not a success in many ways, had changed something fundamental in her.

'Get to the rear, Melyssa, and throw that nylon rope over to the boy, will you?'

His tone was friendly; he called her by her name, but it was a touch commanding.

'He saith "do this", and it is done,' muttered Melyssa under her breath as she struggled with the tightly coiled rope, flinging it up clumsily.

As they walked back up the hill to the villa after collecting her clothes from the beach-cabin, a good two feet apart and in silence, Melyssa hardly knew whether to insist on being taken to the airport for the next flight, or whether to stay on and seek some further opportunity for Emilio to show that other disturbingly desirable side of his personality.

'Now you have had an opportunity to study my plans in more detail, I think we should go to Borgo San Martino and let you see the site up close,' said Emilio.

It was the day after Melyssa's swim. They sat on the terrace in the evening when the scents of lemon and oleander were in the air.

'Yeah, you'll be surprised when you see how big it is,' came a drawling voice from a cane chair. 'I guess it's going to be one hell of a project. Hey, Emil, tell Miss Mosengo about the accommodation bit.'

Sidney lit up and blew cigarette smoke into the night.

'Sidney should know,' smiled Emilio. 'As my secretary, he must have sent off nearly three hundred emails and reports on that part of the project alone. Here,' Emilio pushed the plan sheets across to Melyssa and jabbed at the top sheet. 'Here is my school. This is the best part of the project. Here will live poor boys from ordinary homes, like me – boys who can sing, of course – and here they will have a chance to become opera singers. No fees, no red-tape, a few grants, perhaps, and the best tuition that I can arrange, and peace for them to learn.'

'Provided by you,' smiled Melyssa.

'Provided, as you say, by me. They have the talent; I have the money.'

'And the talent too.'

'And the talent, I suppose. But I have been very lucky. I owe the world a debt. Now, Melyssa, the school is already built. It is finished in most structural respects. What it now needs is the decor and the fittings. I should like that job to be done first while construction on the tower and the theatre continues.'

'And you think it's time that I saw it?' asked Melyssa. 'Yes, so do I. It's not easy to get a clear idea of what a place is like from computer projections and floor plans alone.'

'*Si, si.* Especially as you have done no important work before.' It was the Contessa's voice. With one of her endless cigarettes, she had come silently onto the terrace. Her smile suggested that this comment was a sort of joke, but Melyssa knew there was a sneer behind the jocular tone.

'Emilio,' went on the Countess, 'you had better take this green girl to Borgo *domani* – tomorrow. You don' want to find that you 'ave picked the wrong horse for the job. *Capiche?*

Melyssa, feeling that she was about to make too much of Loredana's ill-natured interruption, but unable to stop herself, snapped,

'I don't see what right you have, Contessa, to carp and criticise the work of "Calypso Designs". You have never seen anything my firm has worked on.'

'Oh, haven't I?' retorted Loredana cryptically. 'Well Emilio hasn't. I know that, *cara*.'

'Oh can it, for God's sake,' drawled the American secretary. 'Why do you have to say things you don't mean about other people?'

Loredana made no response, shrugged her shoulders and drifted back inside the house. Emilio looked at her retreating back, opened his mouth to call after her, thought better of it, and was silent.

'Sorry, Melyssa,' he muttered.

'Aw, she's got out of bed the wrong side, as usual,' yawned Sidney. 'Take no notice.'

What has she got against me? thought Melyssa. She glanced after the Contessa and back at Emilio. She remembered that first impression she had got in London that they were lovers. She *can't* be jealous of me. She can't know about yesterday morning on the yacht. As she turned her thoughts back, she found she just couldn't square Emilio's actions with her with the idea that he was her lover. My first impressions must have been wrong. She had to admit that Emilio had been the soul of polite attentiveness to her: the rich, courteous, friendly employer in the presence of his professional advisor. Not by word or gesture had he betrayed that anything unusual had happened on the yacht. In fact, he had not mentioned that she had been on the yacht at all. It can't be jealousy, thought Melyssa. She's got a down on me for some other reason. Racial prejudice, probably. Well, blow her!

'We shall go to Borgo tomorrow,' said Emilio. 'Then, Melyssa, you can judge the restoration and the plan for yourself.'

Later that evening, unable to sleep in the hot night, and with her brain full of ideas and misgivings, Melyssa had gone out onto the terrace which ran along the side of the villa, forming balconies for each of the bedrooms. She had stood, leaning on the balustrade, when she was aware of voices speaking in Italian from the darkness. She could not make out what was being said, but she recognised Loredana's deep smoker's voice on a pleading note. Then came Emilio's calm tones. The rest of the dialogue was dominated by the Contessa, followed by the sound of a door or French window opening. Emilio's voice was now much clearer,

'*Accommarditi, Lora,*' was what Melyssa heard.

The window closed again with a click and there was silence once more.

Melyssa stared into the heavy night and was startled to feel tears pricking her eyeballs. She was dismayed by the murderous jealousy rising in her heart. She felt, unreasonably, insanely, that it was *her* right to march along to Emilio's bedroom and demand entrance. She wondered if she had the courage to force her way in and hurl the Contessa out into the dark. Instead, she went back in and lay on her bed.

What is happening to me? I seem to be changing into a wild, different person. I'm no longer cool, calm and – and professional. With a rush, the image of two bodies entwined on tousled sheets rushed into her mind – the hot image of wet mouths reaching to each other and fire sweeping across skin and limbs. She felt fingers clasping her own secret parts – her fingers. In her brain there rose up an image of the Black Tower and then it seemed to become Emilio. Dark hands crushed her breasts.

All night long she alternated between the agonies of her infatuation and distressing nightmare. She wondered if her dream was Freudian, in her genes, or a product of stress. The Black Tower was always near her.

'I guess I'm driving,' said Sidney.

It was morning, bright and clear. Melyssa drew approving glances from the American as she appeared in the only dress she had brought from London, the lemony one she had worn at dinner and which was short enough to show off her nice legs. 'You look pretty peachy, Miss Mosengo,' he went on. 'A great sight for a morning's sore eyes.' The same big car that had met her at the airport waited outside. Sidney jumped in and started up. 'Hey! Jump in, dozy!' he called.

'Oh, yes. Right,' replied Melyssa. 'Where's – um – Signor Monza?'

'He went off an hour or two ago. Didn't you hear the motorbike?'

'Oh, that was his bike? Yes, I heard it when I was waking up. I've been slow in getting together this morning. I didn't think – I didn't realise….'

'You didn't realise that Emil rides a motorbike? You think a big-shot ought to go round in a limo? You're thinking of big shots of sixty years ago; John Lennon's Rolls and all that. No, Emil has a passion for bikes. He's got a Harley Street Glide, a new Honda Gold Wing, a classic Moto Guzzi Falcone and a 1970s Norton Commando.' Sidney paused, clearly expecting a gasp of approval from Melyssa. 'A Norton, you know. British. Highly collectable. Difficult to maintain. Eccentric. Goes like the wind – when it goes. That's the one he's taken today.'

'Ah, I thought he'd be waiting 'til…..'

'You expected him to wait while you had a leisurely breakfast. No way, Sister. He gets over to the site to catch a word with the contractors before they begin. They have a morning meeting each day. Hell, he didn't expect you to go to that,' added Sidney kindly, as Melyssa's face fell. 'That's why I'm all ready to take you over. That's why he took the bike and left the car.'

The Bentley purred down the drive. Melyssa sat in front next to Sidney.

'I guess you're wondering why Emil never seems to be caught doing any work. He's working all right. But often at night, and early in the day. He hardly ever sleeps, that baby. Next week, he's recording in Milan. You should come up and get an earful.'

On the drive to Borgo – a short one of barely half-an-hour – Sidney gleaned a lot about Melyssa: her life in Bristol, her background, her partnership with T-ray, her new business, her determination to succeed in a difficult field dominated by a few top pros.

I like taking to him, thought Melyssa; it's as easy as chatting with T-ray. Such a difference in him when *she* isn't around. In her over-wrought state, Melissa found a sympathetic listener soothing. She couldn't help thinking that she wouldn't have enjoyed that run so much if she'd been driven by Emilio. There was too tense a current flowing between them for chit-chat to be easy. Yet she longed to see him again.

'Here we are. You can see the village up there on the hill. Boom! Boom!' cried Sidney. He swept the car in through two ancient ochre-coloured posts some miles after they had left Lucca behind and were nearly at Pescia. A narrow country road, well-surfaced, wound upwards in a succession of tight hair-pins through vineyards and stunted, prolific olive trees. Ahead, the little Tuscan town clung to the hills. Near the top, the car made another turn and passed a flattened area of earth and rock. Melyssa was surprised to see how much hillside had been removed.

'It's so big!' she gasped.

'Yup, quite a sight,' grinned Sidney. Several excavators and heavy trucks were parked on the rocky protrusion. 'Now stand by, Miss Mosengo! That's Borgo over on your left, just as we come round this next corner, and on your right at the end of the excavation, ta-ran-ta-ra! Il *Torre del Purgatorio*! Soon to be Il *Teatro del Torre*, or the Tower Theatre, as I guess we'd call it. Look.'

Melyssa was looking. Her hands clutched the sides of her seat. Her breath came fast.

'But it's….it's…' she started to say. Then she was silent, her heart pounding, her fingers digging into her palms. For the tower on the hill was none other than the black tower of her nightmares. Yes, oh yes, she knew every stone of it. Every fissure of its black column she had seen in dreams.

'Hey, Miss Mosengo, you all right?' cried a solicitous Sidney. 'Gee, I guess I've driven pretty quickly up those hairpins. You'll feel better when we've stopped.'

Grateful that he had mistaken her shock – her ridiculous shock, like something from a creaking horror movie – for car-sickness, Melyssa nodded dumbly. The car came to a halt at the base of the dark tower.

'I'll be fine in a minute or two,' she said faintly.

'Oh good. You're here,' came Emilio's voice. He strolled forward from the construction site. His legs were encased in dark, tight leather – motorcycling gear, Melyssa supposed – and he wore a white T-shirt. Melyssa felt her usual stab of irritation at what she took to be his male vanity, and then the satisfying joy of seeing him again, and then anger at the thought that the Contessa was his lover, then fear when she looked up at the black tower on the hill. The successive emotions gave her face a mobile childlike quality, and she became aware of Emilio's gaze resting for some time on it, and on her elegant figure in the lemon dress.

'Park the car, Sidney,' said Emilio. 'Melyssa, now you will come with me to see what I had planned for you to do when we first met back in London.'

'It's immense,' quavered Melyssa. 'Far bigger than I imagined.'

'Yes, I suppose it is a big area. But remember, apart from the school, which is complete apart from the interior, the accommodation and the theatre, there must be space for parking cars and coaches. There's no parking over in the town. I've got used to it and it doesn't seem so large up here, you know.' He tapped the side of his head.

'Is this where the theatre will be?' asked Melyssa, pointing to the concrete structures at the base of the tower.

'Yes, yes. The theatre construction has started – although it doesn't look immediately obvious. Just ahead of where we are standing will be the semi-circle in front of the building, the orchestra pit and stalls will be within those concrete uprights. The difficult bit has been the foundations because the hill never had a flat top, and because we had to dig deep to protect against earthquakes.'

'Oh, do you get them here?'

'Indeed. We've two small tremors since we began work. Nothing much, but we must make sure. And there are regulations.'

'And the – the tower?' Melyssa could hardly bring herself to utter the word.

'Aha, *Il Torre del Purgatorio*! Well, I have fond boyhood memories of it, but – as you will discover – it is rather a special place.'

'Yes – but….but how did you know about me and the dreams?'

Emilio stared at her.

'Dreams? About what?'

'Oh, no, that's not what I meant to say. Sorry. What did you mean about it being special?'

'Can't tell you yet because I'm waiting for a ruling. But I think you'll be pleased and surprised. It would be more convenient to demolish it, but I'm making it part of the theatre complex. Let me show you over it.'

He turned and led the way. Huge pillars of concrete had been set into the rock. Now she was alone with him again. The workers on the rock wall were preparing steel girders for the middle section of the tower, but were waiting until after her visit. She felt oppressively that she couldn't be natural after what had happened on the yacht.

'Emilio….' She began.

'I know what you're thinking. I behaved badly on the *Buona Fortuna*. But, Melyssa….' He paused for a second. 'Melyssa, do try to take it as a compliment to the most lovely young woman I have ever seen. You and I have known each other in sudden and unusually intimate circumstances, given our brief acquaintance, I realise that.'

'Quite,' said Melyssa. 'You would have as good as raped me, if I hadn't fought you.'

'If I had wanted that – and it is an ugly, ugly word, Melyssa – you could not have stopped me. But I wanted to make *love* to you. And that's not the same thing. And why?' he hurried on, as she was clearly going to interrupt him, 'because *you* wanted me to make love to you. You can't deny it. You were keen. I knew it. I sensed it.'

'I – I wasn't. I didn't….'

'You are not being honest with me. And,' he added, 'you're not being honest with yourself. Look,' he went on, softly, 'I *know* when another person wants love. I'm not inexperienced. You, on your side, are not inexperienced either, surely?'

Melyssa said nothing, but her mind conjured up the inept and inconclusive sexual experiences she had had with Brian in Bristol.

'You are passionate,' said Emilio. 'I felt the fire in your body when we kissed, an answering fire to my own. When I held you, Melyssa, you burnt against me. Then you suddenly rejected me. I can see why,' he said, almost to himself, 'that is why I admit that I behaved badly towards you. You were at a disadvantage.'

'You had no right to touch me up.' Melyssa found herself using the plain language of her girlhood.

'You had no right to trespass on my yacht,' he riposted. His eyes flashed at her, but his expression remained good-humoured, as if to say: If she wants to play games, let her.

'You undressed me,' cried Melyssa, blushing at the memory.

'You had fainted. I was putting you to bed like a child. It was when you woke I realised that I had to make love to you.'

'All right,' said Melyssa. 'Be honest, now the heat's off. Do you mean to stand there and tell me that you still want me, as you put it?'

There was a pause. A crane gave out a rattling further away on the site at the school. Emilio looked into Melyssa's beautiful, clear eyes.

'Surely I have made it clear,' he said. 'I have wanted you since we met.'

Afterwards, when Melyssa was to recall every word of this conversation, she realised that he had said nothing about *loving* her. His talk about "wanting her" and "making love" was not the same. There shot back into her mind the interchange she had overheard from her room between him and Loredana. This convinced her that he was a hypocrite and liar, and instead of taking what he had said to her in the spirit he had meant it, she hardened her heart. This is 2024, for God's sake. Women are free. I am free. Men cannot just seize what they want any more, like – like Donald Trump. But she could not pretend that the tensions between them made the job she had undertaken any easier. All that day, as he showed her the works he was financing at Borgo, she alternated between marvelling at his vision, his commitment and his wealth, and dreading being alone with him. She feared that he might press his attentions upon her again; but mixed with that fear was hope. Somewhere inside her there was one woman's primitive jealousy of another, and an angry hurt. To think that he wanted to add her to his collection, unfaithful to both of them!

'I am sick of 'aving her here, *caro*.' It was the Contessa's deep voice on its wheedling note.

Back at the villa, Emilio had gone to change. Sidney told Melyssa that important guests were expected for dinner that night, and Melyssa, not looking forward to such a thing, was debating in her bedroom what on earth to wear, and wondering if the dress she had worn to Borgo was still fresh enough and suitable, when she heard voices along the terrace.

'Eh? 'Ow long is she going to be here, then? I tell you she is watching everything. She watches me, she watches Emilio – and, my friend, she watches you. Her eyes are like a hawk's. She is probably rubbish at her job, but she is no fool, for *una donna straniera,* that is.'

Melyssa had thought at first that the Contessa must have been speaking to Emilio – a reprise of the conversation she had heard the previous night. It was clear she wasn't, but *who* was whispering with her in the gathering dusk?

'Ah, you gotta do something. You're in this too,' went on Loredana.

'Keep your voice down, you careless bitch!' came a reply. Melyssa recognised Sidney's drawl. That on earth were they talking about? Melyssa had not supposed that the American and Loredana were on private speaking terms, other than their favourite game of back-biting and trading insults.

'I'll say what I like,' snapped Loredana. 'Do you think you could get access to the money without me?'

'Quiet.'

There was a sudden shriek.

'Right! You done it now!' came the Contessa's furious voice again. 'You done it now. You touch me again and see what you get.'

'You're too full of hot air,' came Sidney's drawl. 'I'm gonna stick this pin in you again if you say another word in this villa about the money. How many times have I gotta tell you to be discreet? A few drinks and off you go….'

'All right. All right. You get outa my room,' snarled Loredana.

Melyssa, agog in the dusk, heard no more.

That evening, Melyssa received a different picture of Emilio. She had begun to think she knew him, but now she had surprises. The elderly couple, Ada Pratesi and her husband, who looked after the villa were clearly devoted to him. The catty part of her explained that by pointing out how famous and rich he was. Yet she didn't entirely believe it.

At dinner, one of Emilio's eight guests, Sir Ambrose MacIntyre, the British Consular Attache from Florence and Chairman of the British Institute there, turned to her and said quietly,

'Emilio Monza is an almost unique species: the Italian philanthropist. Most Italians are frankly out for Number One alone.'

'*I'm* not one of his philanthropic concerns, Sir Ambrose,' said Melyssa.

'No, no, of course not. Ha, ha, most amusing,' laughed the silver-haired Attache, taking her comment as a pleasantry. Melyssa bit her lip. What she had said sounded self-centred and ungracious. What a yob I am, she thought, reflecting that she had never spoken to a baronet before.

'No, I meant,' went on Sir Ambrose, 'that this part of the world is full of people Monza has helped in one way or another. Take Pratesi here, for example,' Sir Ambrose gestured towards Emilio's gardener who was assisting Ada by waiting at table, and lowering his voice further – unnecessarily, as Pratesi spoke no English – 'The Pratesis had a child very late in life – a boy – and at twelve he developed a blood disorder. Well, the Pratesi family were not well off enough to jump the list for treatment, so Emilio paid for everything and the boy was given immediate attention in Austria. Completely cured; he's twenty now. Emilio cancelled a lucrative tour engagement to see to everything. It cost him a great deal, I believe. He's a wonderful man, as I'm sure you know.'

'But where,' asked Melyssa, 'does he get all his money? I saw his theatre project at Borgo today and it's a stupendous undertaking. It's not as if he's an industrialist, or Elon Musk, or something like that.'

'Well, no. But the top operatic stars in the world make millions of dollars every year.'

'Building the theatre at Borgo would see off quite a few million, I would imagine,' said Melyssa.

'Some of the cost is his own money, yes, and some was willed towards it by Contessa Frosinone's late husband, and he was very rich indeed. Not one of those industrialists, but a major landowner. But I shouldn't think that accounts more than forty per cent of it. The lion's share has been raised by grants and investments from institutions. Signor Monza is an extremely persuasive man, and the Commune of Lucca and the Florence

Restoration Bureau, Fangilio Transport and Tour Buses, the Tuscan lottery and Italian Monuments have all stumped up.'

'It is in everyone's interest that the scheme works then?'

'Of course. This sort of thing will help put Lucca and Pescia even more on the map and it'll do a lot for tourism. It's rather like the Cheltenham Festival or Stratford-on-Avon. Yes, I'd say it's a bit like the building of the Royal Shakespeare Company's theatre there back in the 'thirties.'

'Where Shakespeare was born. Fine. But this theatre is to be where Emilio Monza was born. Not quite the same,' smiled Melyssa.

'See what you mean,' Sir Ambrose laughed. 'The pardonable vanity of the great artist. But I'm glad it's here, and we can forgive him.'

'Why are Italian Monuments interested?'

'*Il Torre del Purgatorio*, of course. I know that Tuscany is full of mysterious and impregnable towers from San Gimignano to Monsummano, but this tower really is a masterpiece. The family who built it were a violent, ropey lot at the time of Boccaccio and the wars between Pisa and Florence. Borgo was an important town then – one of the foothill gateways on the herding paths. The tower was lived in and strongly fortified. But it was the building of it which fascinates everyone. It is constructed of basaltic granite slabs. Not one of them came from local quarries, and it's estimated that the foundations are thirty feet deep to hold it on the hillside. It seems they wanted it to be black. Apparently,' smiled Sir Ambrose, 'it was built with "watchers on the threshold".'

'Watchers on the threshold?' queried Melyssa.

'Soldiers of the family were buried alive up to their necks in the foundation vaults and left there to die of starvation so that their spirits would stay there and protect the tower against earthquake and attack. It's an old custom in the ancient world. That's how the tower got its name. Assuming those wretches died in despair without due rites, their souls would not reach Heaven; hence Purgatory.'

Melyssa shuddered. Sir Ambrose turned to speak to the diner on his other side, and Melyssa was left with her thoughts.

Throughout the meal she had feared to catch Emilio's eye, but at the same time hoped that a signal might pass between them. With mixed relief and annoyance, she saw that Emilio's guests busied themselves with him, leaving him no time to pay attention to her. Sir Ambrose, whom she found kindly but boring after too long a time with him, turned back to her and, as the dinner ended, led her out onto the terrace for coffee. There he spoke urbanely of Renaissance art, of Tuscan architecture and the cost of staging grand opera these days. He stood with his back to the lit room, and Melyssa, facing him, nodding politely and every now and then saying: 'Quite', 'Good Heavens' or 'Really?' had a view of Emilio lying back in a white leather chair, chatting to some of his guests. How striking he always looks when arrayed against white, thought Melyssa. Her eyes followed the curves of his body from neck to his ankles. Her mind tore back to her experience on the yacht when he, taut with sexual desire, had held her closely to him. She gave a slight, involuntary gasp.

'Eh? What?' asked Sir Ambrose, interrupting the flow of his own rambling academic voice.

'Oh, nothing,' said Melyssa, forcing her mind back to the elderly man in front of her. Oh God, she thought, as he resumed his monologue, I have never felt such yearning for love. I must go to him, when this evening ends. I shall go to him....and let him take me. I want sex now. She felt her teeth grind with suppressed desire as again the image of Emilio's naked body darted in front of her inner eye.

In this disturbing state, and trapped by the talkative Sir Ambrose, who had clearly taken a fancy to her and was no doubt glad to get away from the other guests whom he either did not know, or who spoke little English, Melyssa saw Emilio stand. He smoothed his trousers over his hips and thighs, and bade farewell to three of the people in the room. She saw his smile flash, saw the wife of the Mayor of Borgo caress his neck as she kissed him goodnight.

What is wrong with me? What is happening to me? Surely I can't have fallen in love with him? So out of touch had Melyssa been with her own emotions after the sorry little affair with Brian, her time in teaching and then the year in London building up the business, that she was unable to answer her own questions.

She nearly cried out to him when she saw Emilio look directly towards her – yet there was nothing at all in his eyes as they came to rest in her direction. She then realised that he could probably see nothing on the dark terrace but Sir Ambrose's back.

Eventually Sir Ambrose took his longed-for leave with old-fashioned courtesy, and Melyssa, Sidney, Emilio and the Contessa were free to go to bed.

'Waal, I guess I'm going to hit the hay,' drawled Sidney. 'G'night Emil, Melyssa. Aw-aw-aaaaaw!' He yawned widely and, pointedly ignoring Loredana, made his way upstairs.

Melyssa looked from Loredana to Emilio. The Contessa out-stared her, almost as though forcing her to take her leave. Melyssa said her goodnights in a low voice and left the room. It might have been her imagination, but she thought she caught, at the edge of her vision, Emilio make a movement towards her.

Once upstairs she lingered outside her room, feeling childish, resentful, yet burning with unsatisfied longing. She waited for Emilio to come up in his turn.

I am going to him, she decided, and I'm going to say: You wanted me on the yacht; now take me. I want sex with you because I love you.

Part of her mind thought that little speech sounded ridiculous – like something from a romantic novel – but the real physical yearning, which made every moment without him an agony, kept her looking over the balustrade.

She saw Ada switch off the lights. From a dark spot, she spied Loredana coming up with a hesitant motion which told of her usual heavy drinking, and go into her suite along the corridor. A few moments later Emilio appeared. His jacket was over his shoulder. The passage light shone on the highlights in his hair. Now, now I will go to him….

She was about to show herself when, sick with disbelief, the saw him look at his watch and follow Loredana into her suite. A final light went out and Melyssa was alone in the warm darkness, her silly, girly speech rotating in her brain.

Much later, undressed, she lay while the Tuscan moon played about her. The practical side of her character had told her, more than once, that her infatuation with Emilio was largely chemical, rather than a mystical collusion of souls. And she attempted to remedy this. In her late teens, she had made the discovery that the act of private self-pleasuring in her bed was a great help to her; she believed in the benefits of strong orgasms and had always felt her mood enhanced and her nature relaxed by them when life got difficult and stressful. She had packed the useful private purchase she had found on-line, knowing she might need it in Italy.

Tonight, however, bringing herself to eventual climax had made things worse, for throughout her increasing sexual stimulation, her mind had conjured Emilio's body and his arms about her, and, distracted, she found she could not lose herself completely in her sensations as usual. Nor afterwards did she feel her normal relaxation and satisfaction.

Towards dawn, she tried again to defuse her longings, but somehow her body did not even respond as it had done earlier and orgasm would not come. All she could do was lie, with tired eyes and jumpy unsatisfied nerves, too upset even to cry.

In the morning at breakfast Emilio, seeming not to notice that Melyssa was silent and withdrawn, said,

'We have an interesting day ahead of us, my friends.'

Melyssa sat between the two men at the villa's long table. Loredana, as ever, took her breakfast in bed.

'We sure do,' agreed Sidney, glancing through his glasses at a large diary on the table. 'I'm not sure you're gonna fit it all in, amigo.'

'Of course I am,' said Emilio. 'As long as I arrive in Milan in time for the warm-up session and final rehearsal.'

'As long as you *both* arrive there,' said Sidney, grinning at Melyssa; and he added, 'in one piece.'

Melyssa, thus addressed, looked up from her figs and *pane scuro*.

'Oh, are you going to Milan?' she asked.

'I am,' replied Emilio. 'I have a recording session at La Scala's rehearsal hall. I am singing the tenor parts in "*Carmina Burana*". Not long, perhaps, but technically interesting and needing warm-up, of course. But you, *mia cara Melyssa*, are coming with me, after we have first gone over to the site at Borgo.'

'What are we doing at Borgo today?'

'Aha. Exciting things go on there.'

'Guess,' cried Sidney.

'Yes, guess,' smiled Emilio.

Melyssa, feeling a wet blanket, looked from on to the other. She felt keenly that her mood of depressed introspection and disappointment was a sorry contrast to the boyish good spirits of her host and his secretary.

'Oh, I don't know. I can't guess. What is it to do with? The school or the theatre?'

'Waal,' said Sidney, 'more school than theatre, ain't it, Emil.'

'Yes. Guess, Melyssa.'

How pretty my name sounds from his lips. He seems to say it with a caress. It's true that I've never thought before that my name is like being lovingly stroked when spoken by him. At home it was always Mel or Melly.

'I'll give you a clue,' said Sidney. 'You can fish out your paste.'

'Fish out my what….?

'Paste!'

'What does that mean? Fish out?' asked Emilio, puzzled for a moment by the colloquial English.

'Sorry. For your benefit, Emil, she can get out her paste-pot.'

'Paste-pot, eh?' smiled Melyssa in spite of herself.

'.....and brush,' grinned Sidney. 'And bucket,' he added.

'Oh! You mean we can actually start decorating, wall-papering, painting! Oh, great! You mean it's finished? The school, I mean.'

'It is finished, or perhaps I should say it isn't, said Emilio. 'But today we meet the contractors and take over the shell, as it were. Power is on, water is on, the locks are on.'

'In,' said Sidney.

'In,' said Emilio. 'Why in, not on?'

'Search me, bo,' said Sidney.

'So,' continued Emilio, tapping Melyssa's arm – a touch which sent tremors through her flesh so that the tiny fine hairs on her arm rose as though she had goose-pimples, 'so, you, my interior decorator, are going to the contractors today to meet the man in charge and submit to him those plans for paint, paper, décor, light fittings, flooring and furniture which you researched in London. In short, from today it's all yours – the lecture rooms, the music rooms, the reception foyer, refectory and accommodation. The only part of the building which is already fitted out is the kitchen. I didn't think we'd need a designer to say where to put ovens and sinks and fridges.'

Melyssa gazed at them.

'Excited?' asked Sidney.

'Yes,' said Melyssa – and she meant it.

Now that she could get her teeth into the job at last, some of the unreal and disturbing set-backs of the last few days faded into their proper perspectives. The swim out to Emilio's boat, Emilio's attentions to her, the rudeness of the Contessa, the nightmarish dinner with Sir Ambrose and the night that followed – all fell into their proper positions. All were secondary to her reason for being out here at all.

For the first time since her arrival, Melyssa felt on home ground. How often had she designed interiors for buildings in London? Not on such a scale, maybe, but the principle was the same. She was especially happy to think of all those "before" and "after" photographs she was going to load on her phone, the best of which would appear on the "Calypso Designs" website and on portfolio brochures. Suddenly she felt very fond of T-ray who had started the business and, having forgotten his existence over the last stressful days, got off a text putting him in the picture.

That day, as Sidney had promised, was one of the most exciting of her life. Equipped with a borrowed crash-helmet and clinging on with fearful fingers, for Melissa had never ridden pillion on a motorcycle before, she was whisked to Borgo on Emilio's gleaming Honda GoldWing. The old Norton was deemed far too temperamental for the rapid rush all the way up to Milan which was to follow the meeting with the contractor.

To Melyssa's relief, the contractor (for whom Emilio acted as interpreter) was respectfully and attentively appreciative of her plans and ideas. Feeling confident again, less like an inadequate schoolgirl, Melyssa strode through the marble-floored foyer and on into the interior, the soft leather jacket which Emilio had lent her draped over one arm. Emilio and the contractor smiled and consulted in rapid Italian, conning over Melyssa's folders of specifications and the computer-generated interiors on her lap-top, seeming pleased with all that she had planned.

When hands had been shaken and future dates sorted out, Melyssa swung her long, shapely leg over the seats of the Honda as if she'd been riding high-powered motorcycles all her life, and Emilio swept her onto the autostrada at Montecatini Terme and then, after Pistoia, headed north on the Autostrada del Sole for Milan.

The huge, six-cylindered machine blurred the swiftly passing kilometre posts. Melyssa gasped with apprehension as they roared into the first really long tunnel through the Apennines. Although he had told her that she could sit back relaxed on the thronelike seat and lean confidently on the rear top-box, her arms entwined Emilio's body at speed and every now and then he caught her eyes in one of the wing mirrors and they smiled at each other, united by the exhilaration of rushing through the warm summer air. Once Melyssa screamed into his ear, 'What speed are we doing?' and had clung even harder to him when she worked out that 170 kpm was close to a hundred miles an hour.

In two hours they were threading the busy streets of Milan.

An hour after that, Melyssa sat in the great rooms used by the La Scala company and watched the recording of the tenor parts of "*Carmina Burana*" with the boys' choir of the monastery of San Vincenzo supplementing La Scala's singers. Melyssa, not very knowledgeable about classical music, was thrilled and uplifted by Carl Orff's famous work, and she felt an almost possessive pride at Emilio's effortlessly fine performance.

Once again she noticed how reverently he was treated and how much liked. On only one occasion did that self-regard which she had detected in him at their first meeting come to the surface. At six o'clock the musical director, recording engineer and producer were playing back the afternoon's work. It appeared that Emilio felt he was recorded too much in the background in one section. He insisted with considerable force that the balance be restored in his favour at the mixing stage. Even so, Melyssa's ears told her that musically he was right, and the producer wrong.

Melyssa was happy again as they roared back south after a lovely intimate dinner at the Ponte Nuovo. The GoldWing seemed to peel back the onrushing air like a rocket cleaving the space between the stars, and she felt orchestras singing in her heart in tune with the engine's effortless throb. She laid her head to Emilio's shoulder and let her whole being surrender to the bliss of being with him alone in the night.

I am, just now, completely contented, thought Melyssa.

It was just as well that, as the motorcycle whirled her along the unwinding tarmac, she knew nothing of the misery she was destined to feel in the days ahead.

MISERY

Early summer ripened into a mid-summer of blazing heat, golden-yellow days and warm, caressing nights. Utterly absorbed in the work of decoration and fitting-up of the school building, Melyssa almost forgot her life back in Battersea.

Once a week T-ray rang her to ask how the contract was going. It had been decided that there was no need for him to come out to her, other than for a catch-up visit before work on the theatre began. Recovered from Covid, he was pressing on with jobs on four "Executive" homes in Barnes. He told Melyssa that it was grey and overcast in London, and how brief their heat-wave had been, but at least hosepipe bans were off and people could wash their cars again. Melyssa listened in astonishment as if to tales from another planet.

In her concentration upon the sunny rooms at Borgo, in her joy at being taken there from the villa at Monte Bulciano astride Emilio's GoldWing or beside him in his red Porsche 911 convertible, Melyssa felt that she had her being in a perfect world of satisfaction, absorption and delight.

It was a pity, therefore, that her relations with the Contessa continued to slide downhill. On Melyssa's side there was always a feeling of dread when they met, for Loredana was nearly always drunk and on the edge of being abusive. On the Contessa's side, a dislike of Melyssa was developing into something close to hatred. With Sidney, she quarrelled endlessly and viciously. Melyssa wondered how on earth the easy-going American stood it. She would not have been surprised to see him slap Loredana's face, and wished she had the courage to do so herself.

Only Emilio appeared able to speak to the Contessa without getting a rebuff or an insult – and it upset Melyssa that he seemed to see as much of her as ever at the villa. Never again, however, did Melyssa set out to spy on Emilio, but her instinct told her when he was closeted with the spoilt, shrewish young widow – and it seemed far too often.

One evening, after a day of the burning *scirocco*, when the heat seemed more oppressive than ever, an explosion was near. Melyssa, with more than a certain amount of trepidation, was preparing to drive herself home alone from the tower in the red Porsche.

'Fourth gear's enough. You won't need fifth,' Emilio had told her.

'Do you think I've never driven a powerful car before?' Melyssa had snapped – although, of course, she never had.

God, it's so typical, she had thought. This man always treats me like an incompetent fool.

'Just go easy on the accelerator and brakes. They're pretty instant.'

'I had a car when I was eighteen,' yapped Melyssa, irritated by Emilio's patience. 'It was almost exactly like this one, actually,' she lied. 'So there's no need for you to go on and on.' Melyssa had been regarded as a useful friend in her first year at Bristol university by virtue of her little brown Ford Fiesta. She was in demand for lifts and shopping. She did, of course, realise that her thirteen year old car, bought by her mother for £800, could not really be compared to a £130,000 Porsche 911, but she was damned if she was going to admit it to Emilio.

'Just be careful though, especially when you get off the Aurelia after Lucca and onto the mountain road,' warned Emilio. He pushed back his dark glasses with a half-amused and half-concerned expression as Melyssa, tossing her black curls at him, jammed the Porsche into gear and shot out of the development site onto the hill road.

Melyssa saw him standing there – a tiny image in the rear-view mirror – and stamped her foot on the accelerator.

'You never gonna see that car again, Boss,' joked the foreman, as he joined Emilio at the gates.

'It's not the car I'm worried about,' murmured Emilio, turning back towards the building – more than half regretting that he had suggested this idea to Melyssa. The previous day, he had accepted a lift back with the director of a Lucca company, so had both his Norton and his Porsche on the site. It had seemed sensible for each of them to take a vehicle back to the villa.

Out on the road – the autostrada from Florence to the coast – Melyssa felt Emilio's anxious words rankling in her breast.

'Huh. Don't go out of fourth,' she muttered, not realising that he had meant exactly what he had said. 'Watch the brakes, little woman. He lives in the Stone Age. How dare he?'

Melyssa dragged the lever across the gate and shoved it into fifth gear. Her speed was already in the high seventies and now, as her foot depressed the pedal further, it ran into the nineties. With her mind dwelling on Emilio's condescension, she shot, unaware because the speedo was in kilometres, up to 110mph. Soon she was hooting at the darting vehicles that seemed to be determined to get in her way.

Disaster was not long in coming. A slow-moving Toyota Prius hybrid pulled out to pass a huge and even slower German lorry and trailer just before the turn-off to Altopascio. Melyssa, not used to driving on a two-lane motorway, and coming up at nearly three times the speed of the Toyota, had no choice but to brake furiously. Too late Emilio's words about gentle braking shot into her mind, but the red Porsche, avoiding ploughing into the back of the hybrid by a whisker, skidded across the carriageway as the lorry passed. The Porsche's left front wing swiped the trailer's rear end safety girder and then, with a grinding crunch, swerved onto the pitted gravel beyond the hard shoulder and, in a spray of stones, stalled. Melyssa was jolted forward in her seat-belt, wrenching her neck painfully. The German truck driver, aware only that a flashy red sportscar behind him had rushed onto the hard shoulder, and that it was driven by some rich young woman who couldn't cope with it, shrugged his shoulders and roared on in a cloud of black diesel.

'Oh God! God!' Melyssa kept crying. The pain in her neck was like a knife scoring into her muscles. Her first thoughts were of anger towards the truck driver, the Toyota and Emilio's Porsche – and most of all at the stance Emilio would take: condescending, perhaps smiling. And then the cost of repairs! At no point did she consider how lucky she had been to escape death. Cars raced by while she sat and wept tears of impotent rage.

After ten minutes she felt strong enough to get out of the car and inspect the damage. One headlight had gone. The wing was torn open, exposing the tyre. A deep score ran along the side halfway across the door. The lower paintwork was dented by flying stones.

Melyssa had never been in a road accident and did not know what she should do. Her Italian was nowhere good enough to use her smartphone – even if she had known what number to ring. As usual, as would have been the case back home, the stream of cars whizzed on, their occupants giving her no more than a passing glance of interest.

Taking deep breaths to pull herself together, and still feeling shocked and jarred, she got back into the car and started the engine. It responded immediately, sounding much as it had done earlier, but when she put the car into gear and drove onto the hard shoulder there was a nasty sound of grating and grinding. The steering felt odd and heavy. Clearly something underneath had been damaged.

Melyssa took a grip on herself.

'Where are we?' she said aloud. 'I'm sure we passed Altopascio a few moments ago. Lucca is not far off now. We must get off the autostrada and then we'll see if we can get back to Bulciano on quiet roads.' She referred to the Porsche and herself as "we", as if between them they had done something naughty and must now calm down and not be silly.

'Right,' said Melyssa to herself. 'Right. Into first and onto the carriageway. Anything coming? No. Right.'

The Porsche, now travelling at barely 25mph, instead of 120, clanked on in second gear towards the Lucca exit.

Apart from raised eyebrows from the man in the toll booth, Melyssa excited no comment as her clattering vehicle headed out towards the hills above Via Reggio.

'Oh dear,' sighed Melyssa as her eye caught a red light winking below the sat-nav screen, and her ear tried to decipher a very peculiar squeaking from the front of the car. 'Oh dear. Ha, ha, ha!'

Soon she was laughing hysterically. The steering was amazingly heavy. The squealing had been the left-side tyre shredding on the bent wing as the front wheels turned. It was now flat and the car bumped along in first gear.

By the time the gates of the villa were in sight, smoke was coming out behind her, not that she had noticed, and her laughter had once more reverted to sobs.

As the car spluttered to a halt at the front doors, Melyssa stayed in the driver's seat, her head on the wheel, deeply relieved to have made it back in one piece.

'*O Dio mio!* Look! Look!'

It was the screech of the Contessa.

'This girl! This brainless fool of a black girl! Look what she done!'

Loredana rushed down the steps, followed by Ada, her husband, her son and old Signor Vettuci who had come to drain and clean the swimming-pool. They surrounded the car, all speaking at once.

'*Scema! Madonna! Dio Mio!*' screamed Loredana. She grabbed Melyssa's shoulder. 'You get out! Get out! Come! Out! What you done? What you done to my car? You are a *donna pazza*! You wreck my car!'

Melyssa pulled herself together, and drew her arm across her eyes.

'What are you talking about? It's not your car.'

'This my car, *signorina*. I buy it with my 'usband's money. What are you doing in it?'

'This is Emilio's car!' cried Melyssa, her head spinning.

'Who told you? He didn't,' sneered Loredana – and, of course, now Melyssa thought about it, Emilio had not actually told her who owned the Porsche. She had naturally assumed it to be his.

'Get out of it!' shouted Loredana.

'Look. Look,' cried Melyssa, 'I'm sorry. I'll – I'll pay for the damage.'

'Don' be stupid. You could not pay for the work on this car even if you sell the cheap little company where you work. Hey!' yelled the Contessa theatrically, 'You couldn't afford an *ashtray* for this car!'

Melyssa, realising the truth of these comments, felt her jaw dropping with dismay. There seemed nothing more to say. She got out and ran into the house, trying to muster as much dignity as possible, but failing.

Sidney Gill stepped out of the office next to the veranda doors.

'What the hell....?' He began, but Melyssa tore past him, ran to her room, and threw herself onto her bed, and lay with clenched fists, breathing fast in a state close to panic.

'Where is Melyssa?' asked Emilio some two hours later after his return on the Norton.

'Er, well…. She's all shook up,' said Sidney.

'Yes,' said Emilio grimly. 'I've seen the car.'

'Needs a spot of work, doesn't it? Lady drivers, eh?'

'Ring her mobile,' said Emilio, 'and tell her it's dinner-time.'

When her phone rang, Melyssa had already composed herself and was bitterly regretting her earlier behaviour. Why, oh why, she asked herself in exasperation, do I always have to go and behave like an unsophisticated, inadequate sixth-former as soon as some crisis develops? Why didn't I drive more slowly and carefully? What was I trying to prove? Why did I run up to my room and not face up to Loredana?

Having put on the most alluring item in her wardrobe – a rich, plant-green summer dress with a white stripe which she had bought a week ago in Montecatini, and her chunkiest silver jewellery, so that she looked young, fresh and cool, a lovely girl whose delicate brown skin and lush Afro hair smelt of lemons – Melyssa ventured into the dining-room.

As she crossed the veined *terrazzo* flooring, she felt Emilio's eyes slam into her figure. From the leather chair from which he now rose, his eyes had hungrily absorbed the lilt of her dress, her fine ankles, her flawless calves, her brown arms loaded with her silver bracelets. As his gaze enwrapped her and she knew she detected his dark-lashed arousal, she was uplifted into courage.

'I must apologise once again, Contessa, for the damage I caused to your car,' she said with dignity. She found it almost impossible to address Loredana by name.

'What's that?' asked Emilio.

Melyssa repeated her direct apology once more.

'What are you talking about?' he said, his lips curving into a tolerant smile. 'That's *my* car you're talking about, not Loredana's.'

'Oh!' gasped Melyssa. 'But she told me...she said...'

'You,' said Emilio with ice in his voice, turning to the Contessa, 'you said that to Melyssa. What the hell did you say that for?'

Loredana drew back her head and gave a guttural, hoarse laugh.

'Hah! I only joke, for God's sake! So what? I like to see the girl's face and to get her apology. It made me laugh. I make a joke.'

Melyssa stared at her, hardly able to believe that this – this spiteful Italian had played such a ridiculous trick, and had taken another opportunity to insult her with gibes which she knew were driven by racial hatred. All her cool dignity fled, to be replaced by a red, pulsing anger. She stepped across the room with a swift stride, whisked round the table, stood over Loredana and slapped her full across the face.

'There!' cried Melyssa, impressively towering in her anger. 'There! You spoilt, selfish, vicious woman! Ever since we met, yes, ever since that night in London at the Dorchester you have insulted me, sneered at me, doubted my ability to do my work, berated me for being a person of colour, for being young! And now, now you start playing games that a five-year old would consider babyish! What are *you,* I might ask? A nobody who swanks around using the title of a husband long dead, a woman who *knows* nothing except how to waste money, and who *says* nothing but ill-natured insults! *And,'* shouted Melyssa, before anyone could stop her, 'who can *do* nothing but drink, drink, drink because your life is a wasted, empty mess!'

Unaware that while she was speaking she had raised her arm again as if to strike the Contessa once more, Melyssa stood over Loredana shaking with fury. Loredana, who had shrunk defensively down to the table level, squirmed unsteadily to her feet and looked at the others. Then, without a word, she moved to the door. Melyssa was horrified to see that great tears were coursing down her cheeks, one of which was already coming up in red, ugly wheals. With a low wail, the Contessa then rushed from the room.

There was a dreadful silence.

'Waal,' came Sidney's voice at last, 'you gave it to her, sister, and then some! She's bin asking for that.'

'No, she did not asked to be assaulted,' said Emilio.

Calmer now, Melyssa turned to face him. Something in his voice arrested her attention.

'She did not,' repeated Emilio. 'You have been in this house less than a month, Melyssa. You have no right to say such things to the Contessa, let alone hit her. Your behaviour was bad. I cannot believe that you don't know how to conduct yourself in decent society. You are, as we say, *maleducata,* Melyssa. I shall not allow this nonsense to go on. This is not what I expected when I drew up my contract with your firm.'

Like someone who has received a glass of water full in the face, Melyssa stood staring at Emilio. *Maleducata!* She knew only to well what a devastating criticism he had levelled at her. That he was furious was plain; the sides of his nose were pinched and his brows contracted.

Before she could speak again, he had followed Loredana from the room.

The suspicion – no, the certainty – that Emilio and Loredana were lovers bit into Melyssa's mind like a corrosive acid. Grotesque though it seemed to her, Melyssa had to admit that the Contessa had known Emilio for a long time, was closer to his age, spoke his language and was, if not a great beauty, a stylish woman by Italian standards. She herself had know Emilio for less than a summer, was foreign, young, black and – let it be admitted – prickly, touchy and often ungracious. Those faults she saw in herself seemed to Melyssa to be magnified when she considered them through Emilio's eyes. She writhed inwardly as she counted off, one by one, the ill-bred, naïve, discourteous and foolish things she seemed to have said since their first meeting. What a silly little brat he must think I am, she sighed to herself. I had my chance with him and I threw it away. And what did he mean when he mentioned the contract? Oh God – bad enough to lose his friendly interest, but to lose his good opinion of my work….. At least I thought I could keep his respect for my professional skills.

From that evening onward, Melyssa decided that she must throw herself one hundred per cent into the next phase of her work. The school was nearing completion of its fitments and the decoration designs of the theatre and the *Torre del Purgatorio* itself were due next. She had spent countless nights working on layout drawings, computer projections and suggestions for colours and décor. Yes, her flair for this part of the project would win him round. He would see that in her own way she was as much of an artist as he was.

Next morning she dropped into Sidney Gill's office.

'Morning, Melyssa. You slept the sleep of the just, I hope,' cried the secretary.

'Sidney,' said Melyssa, rebutting any attempt at badinage, 'how do I go about staying in or near Borgo?'

'What?' asked Sidney, pulling off his spectacles.

'You heard,' snapped Melyssa.

'Waal,' drawled Sidney, 'You know your mind, if you don't mind my pointing it out. You want to leave this lil' ole home-from-home then?'

'I will not remain in this house a single day longer,' replied Melyssa. 'There is no possibility of the Contessa and me getting over what happened last night, and….'

'Oh hell,' interrupted the secretary. 'I shouldn't lose sleep over *that.* I guess and reckon she's bin crying out for what you gave her. People shouldn't ask for what they don't like when they get it.'

'Will you let me finish?' continued Melyssa icily. 'I was going to say that whatever the Contessa feels about my remaining in the villa here, it is ludicrous that I am based over twenty miles from my place of work.'

'Why ludicrous? Folk commute fifty miles in and out of L.A.'

'I have no car here. There is no station at Borgo, so train's no good. I am dependent on Signor Monza for transport on his motorcycle or in his car. I want to be nearer the site, and I want you, as Signor Monza's secretary, to arrange that I, Signor Monza's interior designer, am booked in somewhere nearer the site, and I want it done *now*!'

'Gee whiz, you sure do spill a mouthful when you get steam up, and I guess you speak beautiful English too. No need to shout. I'll fix it. Okay? But you won't find a place in the village of Borgo itself. I'm sure of that. Montecatini has loads of hotels and boarding-houses though. *Pensiones,* they call those. I guess you don't want a five-star hotel, right?'

'No, no. It needs to be fairly cheap.'

'Right. But I'll jest say, Melyssa, that the only places I know of that are not expensive won't be like the Ritz.'

'As long as wherever it is has a bed and provides a meal at night – that's all I want.'

'Oke, sister. Regard it as done.'

Sidney was as good as his word. Within three hours of her request, Melyssa, her things packed, was sitting in a taxi on her way to the Pensione Pompeii e Alda in Montecatini Terme, an easy fifteen minute bus journey down from the site at Borgo, the bus leaving from the bottom of the road.

And so Melyssa's self-imposed exile from Emilio's villa began. Every morning she rose with the other guests at the *pensione* and took breakfast with them in the dark-painted, shaded room at the back of the house – a breakfast which never varied, consisting as it did of one sweet roll, one slice of *pane scuro,* one foil-wrapped pat of butter, one plastic mini-tub of apricot jam and a cup of *cappuccino.* The Pompeii did not run to metal knives, nor to china plates, so Melyssa got used to having her breakfast from disposable plastic and paper. It was very different from the eggs, *prosciutto*, peaches, melons and seeded loaves of the house by the sea.

Every evening Melyssa returned from Borgo San Martino on the bus and took the short walk to the *pensione* in time for supper – again an unvaryingly cyclical meal served in the dark dining-room. *Spaghetti al sugo* went on to a piece of meat, often veal, and ended with *gelato*, usually a *tutti frutti* in bright colours. No one spoke to Melyssa – a tall, single, foreign, black girl – and she spoke to none of her fellow guests. These were elderly Italian couples of modest means who stayed for a week or less to take the famous spa waters of the town. They had bright, black, pin-pointed stares which were fixed sharply on Melyssa from the moment she entered the room to the moment she left.

Her bedroom had deep, wooden-slatted shutters, but no air-conditioning, and as the August temperatures climbed into the high 'thirties, she lay panting and unable to sleep, while the endless scream of Lambrettas, horns and hoarse insistent voices poured into her little room from the canyon of the main street at the end of the road.

At Borgo, as the architectural work on the theatre came to an end, and the interior progressed, Melyssa ran into more and more difficulties. Part of these were with Emilio.

'Why on earth did you leave the villa?' he had asked on the first morning.

'If you don't know, I'm sure I can't tell you,' said Melyssa, hurt that he had not come after her into Montecatini when Sidney had informed him that she had gone.

'It makes it difficult for me to consult you,' he had replied mildly.

'None of my London clients expects me to go back and live with them after the day's work,' Melyssa had snapped tartly. After that he said no more about her residence at the Pensione Pompeii. However, far from looking downcast at her decision, as she had expected, or at least repentant, he seemed amused, and she was very annoyed on those mornings when he greeted her with a frankly derisive grin after she had slogged up the dusty hill-track from the bus stop on the main road.

Yet even the grins were becoming less frequent now, for there was something definitely wrong with the work going on at the complex, and that had nothing to do with Emilio.

On three occasions materials had been found vandalised. Windows, chosen by Melyssa in 'phone consultation with T-ray and newly installed, were found smashed. Once a light Piaggio three-wheeled pick-up truck had been inexpertly set alight. Emilio grew worried that some sort of local opposition to the theatre was growing, and yet there seemed no reason why it should do so, and there was never any clue as to who was behind the outrages.

As if this were not bad enough, Melyssa's plans were getting a rough ride from the engineer and foreman, Signor Bertini. Melyssa had spent hours on her lap-top working in the darkness of her little room preparing sketches and plans for the auditorium décor and lighting. Bertini, with Emilio by his side translating, had proceeded to rip her ideas to pieces. On talking about this to T-ray on her 'phone, his opinion was that the foreman was a typical Italian racially-prejudiced chauvinist who couldn't stomach a woman giving orders, and who certainly had no belief that a woman could grasp complex ideas.

The three of them sat in Bertini's sunny caravan with a noisy air-con plant humming, after the foreman had arrived in his Lancia.

'What is he not happy about?' asked Melissa, noting Bertini's drawn-down mouth and frowning forehead.

Bertini stabbed at the paper designs, one after another, with a stubby finger, muttering .

'He says that the sight-lines are all wrong in the front-of-house plans,' translated Emilio.

'How can they be? From where?'

'From much of the upper part of the theatre. He says your boxes stick out too far and your hanging lamps would block the view of the stage from the gallery.'

She seized the drawings of the upper theatre section. Oh God, it was true. The art-deco light fittings she had specified – quite remarkable and grandly huge, shipped over from a major lighting firm in London, after Melyssa had seen them on a web-site in a theatre in Chicago, specified for lighting the auditorium at the interval and before curtain-up, would indeed create a sight-line barrier between patrons of the gallery and the stage.

'Pah!' snorted Bertini, which needed no translating.

'I – I will look into this at once,' stammered Melyssa. How on earth did I make that slip? she asked herself. Oh Jesus, how stupid can you get? Now everything else I've done will be questioned and doubted.

'Signor Bertini wants to know why you have designed a fly-tower of only six metres high in the base of *Il Torre* itself.'

'You told me yourself that you wanted to incorporate the black tower into the original plan. It would be a wonderful use of its space if part of your stage area ran into its base. The height would give a production the opportunity to use large flying scenery. Lifted by electric motors in the tower you could have skies with cloud machines, painted buildings like sky-scrapers, big cliffs, the works.'

After he had translated this, Emilio then gave Melyssa Bertini's reply.

'He says it would make more sense if you had remembered that there was no longer a second floor in the tower, so the fly-hoist area could be, and should be, at least ten, if not fifteen metres high. More flats could then be stored up there. He asks if you have not studied the similar layout of your Olivier Theatre at the National in London.'

'No, I haven't!' cried Melyssa. 'Okay, okay, we'll use the rest of the height inside the tower. I didn't *know* there was no second floor, because you never told me there wasn't. You only gave me exterior diagrams, remember? I also warned you in London, Emilio, that I knew little of theatre design, but you said it didn't matter – the concept was the main thing.'

Bertini looked on, smiling sarcastically at this outburst.

He did not understand what was being said, but he could see that this young foreigner was exasperated and flustered. He stood and drew Emilio to one side. Had he not told Signor Monza that his own cousin, Giorgio, would have made a much better job of the design? Had he not reminded Signor Monza that the greatest designer in Italy lived at Fiesole, only thirty kilometres away? Had he not told the Signor that a young black girl, still wet behind the ears, would make disastrous mistakes? Was it not lucky that he, Bertini, was on hand to point out these things before there was no turning back?

'Look, I'll redraw the back stage area tonight,' cried Melyssa – only too aware that she was being talked about. 'I'll get it right for tomorrow's meeting.'

'Yes. Fine. Fine,' replied Emilio.

'Well, what was he saying just now? He was disparaging me again, wasn't he?'

'Oh, no. It was nothing. Just some general points. You get back to the drawing-board and see if you get us another computer-projection.'

From that meeting onward, Melyssa felt that she was engaged in a long, personal battle against the Italian engineer and foreman. He now scrutinised her drawings, her workings on her lap-top, and her stock and materials estimates with great suspicion, insisting that Emilio pass every item.

Melyssa came to dread the hot, daily meetings in the works caravan. Emilio was kind to her, true. But she felt that she had forfeited a little of the trust he had put in her expertise. The atmosphere of dislike and contempt generated by Bertini seemed to have spread to the workmen on the site. They expressed their derision, or so it seemed to the harassed Melyssa, by openly wolf-whistling or laughing at her.

'Hey! *Bella*! Kiss! Kiss me!' they would call out.

'How dare they!' she raged to Emilio.

'Take it as a compliment,' he smiled. 'This is Italy, and they do find you attractive.'

Almost every day Melyssa was pinched or ogled on the bus to and from Montecatini. Once, walking back to the Pompeii, two youths mounted the pavement on their electric scooters and had driven slowly next to her, fondling her bottom and making sucking noises. She had had to run for the *pensione*.

Long evenings in her lonely bedroom, hot, with indigestion as often as not, and forced to re-draft her drawings and specifications after annoying difficulties getting a suitable charger with the correct plug to charge up her laptop and, via its USB socket, her phone, the lack of sleep, monotonous tourists' food, the atmosphere of suspicion among her fellow guests and of derision at Borgo – all combined to take their toll on her.

Gradually she began to loathe her existence. Emilio, almost as if to punish her for her mistakes and behaviour, seemed to treat her with no more punctiliousness than he showed to any other person on the workforce. He translated Bertini's endless complaints and queries and also Melyssa's weary, defensive and snappish replies. He no longer smiled when he saw her foot-slogging up from the bus-stop. What interest he had felt in her at the outset of her visit seemed to have melted away.

The Porsche had been repaired, but he never offered her a lift.

On one particularly baking day, about which the morning news had commented as proof of climate change affecting the Southern Mediterranean countries and making them like North Africa, Emilio, Bertini and Melyssa were once again inside the caravan dealing with the foreman's complaints over Melyssa's choice of seat coverings for the theatre. There was the sound of a large car crunching to a halt over dry stones outside. The caravan door opened, and there was Loredana. Behind her, by the car, stood Sidney. Emilio got to his feet, nodded at Bertini, went to the door and put his arm across Loredana's shoulders. He led her outside – not before Melyssa had glimpsed the Contessa's vaunting grin. Bertini tapped Melyssa on the arm.

'*Eh, eh – senta, signorina – queste porte*….,' he began, while Melyssa ached to fling open the caravan door to see what *they* were up to.

Whatever face she put on it, Melyssa's infatuation with Emilio was deeper than ever. Sometimes on the surreal sloping stage of the theatre, with several hundred empty seats looking on, Emilio's dark-fringed eyes flashed with such boyish enthusiasm as he expressed his vision for the opening work and its staging, that she longed to seize him in her arms. When sitting together in the balcony looking down upon the stage and the aisles, their heads close together, poring over a page of design drawings, or sharing a lap-top to check suppliers and projections, her eye was so drawn by the curly hair on his neck, by the ripple of his forearm as his hands turned the pages or tapped on the keys, and she was so aware of the aphrodisiac scent that he carried with him, it took an effort not to grasp him and bury her head in his chest.

Once, when directing her attention to some fitments in the ceiling, he had lifted her chin to point her gaze at the right spot. Their lips had come close, so close, that she felt the gentle brush of his breath. He had held her to him for a second and the feel of his body had electrified her.

In the *pensione*, at night, she dwelt on these things as she lay naked on her hot bed. Round and round her thoughts careered. Sometimes she pictured the ways in which they would make love. So far from being a submissive girl, lying still, grateful to be an object of his sexual gratification, she far more often saw herself as the dominant one, astride him while he entered her from below. Her own solo pleasures nearly always took this form these days; she knelt, sitting on her heels, her device in hand, and imagined his fascinated gaze looking up at her while she climaxed. There was a sort of bliss in looking forward at night to these fictional scenes, but she was aware that her actions did not satisfy or subdue her sexual cravings for him, but rather intensified them.

And now Loredana had calmly walked into the caravan, and he had gone to her like a lap-dog.

'*Eh, eh, eh,*' Bertini was bleating. Melyssa realised how much she disliked this Italian habit of trying to attract attention.

'Yes, what?' she said, turning back to him.

'You ees *stupida*,' he cried, jabbing at the computer screen in front of him. She had slaved at this projection and design for two long evenings at the *pensione*. '*Dove e l'uscita?*'

Melyssa stared at him. There was no one to translate for her.

'*Dove e l'uscita? Eh, eh, dove? La? La?*' He stabbed again at the screen, and then took up her design on paper and jabbed at that.

'What are you talking about?' cried Melyssa, forcing her mind back from the Contessa and Emilio outside the caravan. She looked at the drawings, but nothing in them seemed to warrant Bertini's agitation. Not understanding him, she did not appreciate that he had not found the exits on the theatre stalls plan, and was asking where they were. Melyssa had not, in fact, shown them on her plans nor in her projection.

'*Eh? Eh? Dove?*' snarled Bertini.

'What?'

'*DOVE!*' shouted Bertini. And then, as Melyssa continued to stare at him, he cried, 'Pah!' and tore her accompanying illustration – a drawing she had slaved over – into four pieces and threw them on the floor. *'Pazza,'* he muttered under his breath. Melyssa, not quite catching the rest of the mutter, nevertheless knew that he had made a comment about her skin-colour.

She jumped up, pushing over the table. She wrenched open the caravan door. Behind her she heard, '*Eh, eh, eh....?*' But took no heed. In the back of the car, Emilio and Loredana were sitting together and looking at something on the Contessa's lap. Melyssa bent down and glared in at the open window. She shouted something at them, she hardly knew what. Further away she was conscious of Sidney stamping on a cigarette butt.

I can't stand any more, she screamed inwardly. I *won't* bear this any longer!

The *pensione*, the elderly spa-drinkers, the apricot jam, the leering youths, the dusty walk, Bertini and his bleat, her inadequate plans and designs, the heat and Emilio – oh, Emilio and that bloody, bloody bitch of a Contessa – rushed into a ball of seething loathing in her gut. With a set face she walked unsteadily downhill. Voices were behind her.

She marched quickly along the road. At the stop beyond Borgo she caught a bus. At the *pensione* she packed. She caught the afternoon stopping train to Florence, took a room for the night at the Anglo-Americano hotel, found the right platform for the airport express, boarded the mid-morning relief flight from Galileo Galilei at Pisa, landed at Heathrow before tea-time, crossed London by taxi to Paddington, and at nine o'clock rang her parents' doorbell in Bristol.

'Melly!' Mrs Mosengo cried, opening the door, 'What's – what's happened?'

But Melyssa was running upstairs, still dusty from her travels, and had hurled herself onto her old girlhood bed. There the pent-up misery of weeks overcame her in a great torrent of sobbing which seemed almost to shake the little house.

Eleven o'clock.

Melyssa sat up in the soft bed in the familiar room at Castleton Road. How small a room it seemed. There was a tray on her lap. In her childhood Peter Rabbit egg-cup was a brown shell. Mrs Mosengo had thought that a boiled egg and soldiers, with good sweet tea, would, as a late supper, sort Melly out. And she was right – they had. Melyssa leaned back on four pillows and gazed at the wallpaper of grasses and daisies. She had nearly started on her old game of counting the flowers when there was a tap at the door.

'Melly, dear, I've come to get the tray. Are you feeling better?'

'Mum, you and Dad have been wonderful. I barge in late in the evening, rush upstairs and you ask me no questions, make no comments. You just let me have my cry out and then got me some tea.'

'Do you want to talk to us now? I mean, we'll wait 'til morning if you'd rather…..'

'No Mum. I'll try and explain everything and why I'm here instead of Italy. Give Dad a call. Why don't you perch on the edge of the bed?'

Mrs Mosengo called downstairs, then moved the tray onto the top of the wicker clothes basket, patted down the counterpane and sat. Abraham Mosengo appeared in the doorway, his spectacles in his hand. They looked fondly and quizzically at the daughter who they often felt they did not really know. Melyssa seemed oddly sophisticated as she lay back against the pillows.

'Oh, Mum, Dad, I really do like the feel of these bedclothes.' It was strangely pleasing to feel the weight of a duvet and a counterpane on her legs. At Montecatini she had not been able to bear even a bed sheet at night.

'Is that job over?' asked her father, sitting down on the other side of the bed, and patting his daughter's hand.

'The Italian one? No, Dad, it isn't. Or rather, it is for me. I'm not going back to Borgo to work on it.'

'But why not?'

'You know that postcard I sent you? The one from Montecatini Terme?'

'Oh yes,' said her mother. 'A lovely place it looked. I didn't know they'd put you up at a hotel. Must have been swish.'

'They didn't put me up. I put myself up, and the place I was at wasn't at all swish, Mum. The picture on the card wasn't my hotel; I just grabbed the card from a shop. Do you remember what I wrote on it?'

'Er, what? You mean you wished T-ray was out with you? Yes, I remember. You and T-ray: brother and sister coping together.'

'Yes. Well, I was sort of right. I told him before I left that I didn't think I could handle a job like that on my own – and I couldn't. I know he's had lots of work in London – and that's great for Calypso – but I needed moral support, and he's only come out once in a month.'

'Oh, Melly,' said Mrs Mosengo. 'You've got something to tell us, haven't you? Did it all go wrong?'

'It did.'

Melyssa was about to launch into a description of her ghastly recent month with Bertini, the wrong choice of auditorium lights, the lack of exit doors, the seat coverings, but she paused, unwilling to let her parents know what an inadequate she had been. Instead she touched on the other disturbing – perhaps more disturbing – feature of her time in Tuscany.

'I – I met a man.'

There was a brief silence. Abraham and his wife looked at each other with raised eyebrows. Their complicit gaze seemed to affirm that they might have expected something of that sort.

'Yes,' went on Melyssa. 'It was Signor Monza. You know, the singer who had planned to build a theatre there. I phoned and told you about him and our meeting with him in London before I left.'

'And you fell in love with him, dear girl?' Her mother's voice was soft.

'I think I did,' replied Melyssa, equally softly, but not knowing whether her nightmarish sexual infatuation counted as actual love.

'And,' went on Mrs Mosengo, before Abraham could speak, 'there was another woman, and he couldn't make up his mind.'

Melyssa looked sharply at her mother. Like most children, she believed that her mother and her generation were hopeless outdated innocents, quite unaware of such things as violent sexual longing. With a slight shock she realised that her mum was no less shrewd than herself, perhaps more so.

'Aha,' said Abraham. 'And did he try anything on? Something that upset you? Something that wouldn't have happened if your brother had been out there with you?'

'Well, not really,' said Melyssa, wondering what her father would say about the happenings on the yacht. 'But it's not just him. In fact he is the nicest person I met out there. He's got an American secretary called Sidney, and he's quite nice too. He's very funny, and I wouldn't be surprised to find out that he's gay. He has that sort of waspishness, but is witty with it.'

'Gay guys can be very pleasant,' said Mrs Mosengo, again causing Melyssa to re-assess what her mother might or might not know about life.

'But Emilio has a cousin......'

'You call him Emilio?' interjected Abraham.

'Oh yes. We're pretty informal, you know. But I was going to say, Emilio has a sort of cousin by marriage who is a horrible woman in every way. She's about his age – perhaps a year or two younger – and we just don't get on. She's often drunk, she's racially prejudiced against people like us. We don't get on at all.'

'Is she the "other woman" in the story?'

'Yes, I think so,' replied Melyssa. 'And I can't understand why. She's rich because she's the widow of a well-off Count, and she dresses in a classy way, I suppose. Very expensive outfits and all that. Calls herself the Contessa. But she's shrill, she's vulgar and spiteful; a horrible person, and I hate her.'

'But she isn't involved in the job at the theatre, is she?'

'No, no. Well, I don't think so. Except she's convinced I'm not up to the work, and I know she thinks the whole project won't come off. I've heard her say so. And, and the other person I really hate is called Bertini. He's a little, fat Italian in charge of the site. He buys, you know, materials and he oversees the contractors, like a sort of bursar or foreman, I suppose. Well, I made a little mistake at the beginning, and he's held it against me ever since. Not that I think his opinion counts for all that much. Emilio always listens to my ideas. But I suspect, because I don't know for certain, that he listens to Loredana's too; that's the cousin's name, by the way. She isn't actually involved in the build, so…..'

Now that her tongue was loosened and Melyssa was talking freely, she was disposed to minimise what had happened to her in Italy. And, after all, what *had* happened? Recited baldly like this, it seemed as though she was making a self-dramatising fuss about nothing. As if listening through her mother's ears, she re-evaluated the last two days, and asked herself: well, what *have* you come home for? She suddenly felt a complete fraud. She had suffered no physical harm, no hardship – unless the food in the *pensione*, which many tourists found acceptable, counted. She had had some arguments and disagreements at work with Bertini. But then Bertini had been quite correct to task her for mistakes she had made, even if he was theatrical and tiresome about it. As for the Contessa – well, so what if she was prejudiced and rude? She was no real part of the project, and need never be seen again when the job was over. That left Emilio.

Ah, that was another matter.

Emilio.

Melyssa felt that she could not gloss over the feelings he had aroused in her, so she made up her mind not to tell her parents any more about him.

'Well, you sleep now, my girl,' said Abraham, going to the door. 'I'll take the tray down.' Carrying it in front of him, he left Melyssa's room and padded downstairs. Mrs Mosengo kissed her daughter's brow and followed him. After a few minutes looking at the wall-paper, Melyssa put out the light and slept.

Next morning at ten she was still sleeping, drugged and exhausted by her unexpected whirlwind journey. Downstairs, Mrs Mosengo was on the phone to T-ray and, swearing, T-ray was telling her of the difficulties of dropping everything so he could rush back to Bristol.

A white vault, freshly painted. Searing lights in a necklace of flame just out of vision. Three doorways, black against the white. Melyssa, aware of cold limbs, has to choose between the three doors. Above her, around her, the black tower bursts from the ground like a rocket. Her dilemma is inside its base. Three doors. Inside one is a ramp. It leads to a sharply sloping stage. Dare she take it? The audience out there waits. Her legs are leaden. There are hundreds of faces staring. Inside the second door she glimpses two dark figures hiding round the lintels. Through the third she dare not go – dare not even look. She notices the skulls of the buried watchers at ground level near it. The vault is growing smaller. The black tower's weight is crushing it. Rocks are falling, tapping round her......

Tap, tap. Mrs Mosengo knocked at the bedroom door. After ten. Time Melly got up, surely?

'Melly dear. Would you like some breakfast?'

'Oh, oh! Mum? Yes – er, yes. Of course. Thanks.' Melyssa struggled into a sitting position and shook her head to clear it. The Black Tower! She had dreamt again about it, but, now awake, couldn't remember the details.

'Would you like a sausage? Or a kipper? Or bacon? You didn't eat much last night.'

'Just some orange juice, if you've got some in for Dad, black coffee and – and perhaps a piece of toast, Mum.'

As she gave this request, it occurred to her that it was a weekday and that her mother would normally be at work by ten o'clock.

Mrs Mosengo went down stairs shaking her head at the tiny breakfast her daughter wanted: what nourishment was there in black coffee and a slice of toast and orange juice? Luckily Abraham always liked orange juice for breakfast, so there was plenty in the fridge. Then she heard Melyssa calling again,

'Mum! Mum – why aren't you at work?'

She turned on the stairs and called back up,

'I rang the Health Centre. I said there was a problem in the family and I would be in late morning. I just must hear more about why you've come home so suddenly. I don't want to pry, but….' And then, still half-way down the stairs, she remembered she had a message for Melyssa. 'Oh, Melly, I rang Rebecca earlier and told her you were visiting. I thought she'd be cheerful company for you until T-ray gets here. She's asked you to lunch, so you've got two or three hours to get ready.'

Lunch? thought Melyssa. Oh yes, it's the school holidays. Dear Rebecca. We have so little in common these days. Do I *really* want to go? Aloud she called down,

'Ring her back, Mum. Tell her I'll pop round, but I definitely don't want a lot to eat. I'll be down in a few minutes.'

Melyssa admired herself for speaking firmly, clearly, for now she was standing she felt shaky, tearful and vulnerable, like an oyster ripped from its shell wobbling on a plate. What have I done? Can one walk out on a contract? What will Emilio do? Above all, what will he think of me? What will T-ray say? What on *earth* have I done? Oh, I want to be near Emilio! I miss him so.

Suddenly, standing in her girlish old bedroom, Melyssa had a fierce stab of longing for the blinding sunlight and warmth of Italy – yes, even for the dusty table in Bertini's caravan, if only she could be see Emilio each day. Not surprising, she thought, that I'm attracted to it all, now I have left it; I *am* half-Italian. Yes. I've got to speak to Mum about that.

She pulled back the curtain. In the distance the ginger suburban houses wound away towards the main road. Physically aching, Melyssa washed then pulled on her jeans and shirt. Here his fingers touched. Here he kissed me. I loved sitting with him in the half-completed theatre more than anything else I have done in my life. And he *did* feel something for me. I know he did. Was I jealous of Loredana for nothing? Will I ever know?

The thought of descending to the kitchen filled her with a sort of horror; she knew her mother would want to question her and hear more than she had told. Mrs Mosengo's voice came up the stairs.

'It's ready, dear.'

Breakfast over, Melyssa, having avoided interrogation so far about "the man" she admitted she had met, decided to try for an answer to her own burning curiosity about what Emilio had told her concerning her real father and her birth.

'Mum,' she said, pushing her coffee cup away from her, 'why did you never tell me about Raffaello?'

There was a crash. Mrs Mosengo had let a plate slip through her fingers. She had slumped against the kitchen sink with a look of wild fear. She stuttered,

'W - what? Who?'

'Raffaello, Mum. Come on. My real father.'

'Oh, Melly, no. No. How did you....? When.....? I – I never wanted you to....'

'....never wanted me to know. Yes, Mum, I realise that. I didn't know until T-ray and I were told we were only half-brother and sister about a month ago.'

'A month ago! But who told you?'

'Our employer, Emilio Monza. T-ray and I were absolutely zonked for a moment, but of course it explains why he's so much darker than I am. I'd sometimes wondered about that. And, Mum, it made me love Dad even more. To think what he did for you, and for me just a month or two old.'

'Your father! Oh thank God he's at work, bless him.' Mrs Mosengo sat at the table opposite Melyssa and drew a hand across her eyes. 'Your stepfather, I should call him, is a saint. Oh, Melly, it was just awful back in 1995. I really thought that grief and worry would kill me. Poor Raffaello. It was MDS, a cancer of the blood, they said. They wondered about a bone marrow transplant, after a couple of blood transfusions, but it had gone too far. It was so – so dreadful….' Yolanda Mosengo stopped and stared back nearly thirty years. For a long minute she seemed to have forgotten Melyssa's presence. Then she rallied, picked up the halves of the broken plate, and said loudly, 'And just *how* did Emilio Monza know about me and Raffaello? And what the hell's it got to do with him?'

'What was Raffaello's other name, Mum?'

'His family name was D'Andrea. Why?'

'Emilio Monza's real name is D'Andrea. Monza is only a stage name. His father Giovanni and Raffaello's father Frederico were brothers. Raffaello – my father – was his uncle's son. I'm Emilio's first cousin twice removed, I think.'

There was another silence full of questions and feelings.

'Is T-ray very upset?' asked Mrs Mosengo.

'No. I think he's glad that you and Dad are his parents. I think a big part of him is grateful about Emilio and my – my real father. It's how Calypso got the contract. Emilio wanting to put out work for a family member, as it were.'

Again there was a silence. Mrs Mosengo was Yolanda Cavendish once more, wildly in love with the Italian language student whom she had taken to live in her flat. Melyssa's questions had had an extraordinary effect on her. And one emotion she felt was guilt.

'Mel, I *should* have told you. But, you see, Raff and I never married, so you were what people would call a bastard – not that that matters these days, of course. But at the time......'

'It's a romantic tale, Mum, and I am really glad to know about it. And it changes nothing about today, except having the nice effect of making you tons more interesting in my eyes than just plain old mum working at the Health Centre!'

Daughter and mother looked at each other and laughed. Then Melyssa came round the table and they hugged each other. All would be well.

'You know, I wonder about my old photo and who is in it,' said Mrs Mosengo.

'Which photo?'

'The one on the bookshelf in the sitting-room; up on the third shelf. Let me go and get it.'

Mrs Mosengo disappeared into the next room and Melyssa prepared to go upstairs and get fully ready before going out to Rebecca's. Her mother returned and took the photo frame to the window. In it was a group of eight: an old man with white hair, a short woman in black, two middle-aged men and, between them, a pretty woman in her early forties. A younger woman knelt at the front on the left, a very good-looking youth in round sun-glasses was by her side and a little boy of nine or ten, in shorts, sat cross-legged on the right of the shot.

Melyssa gazed at it closely.

'Raffaello's family?'

'Yes. He gave it to me in 1993, not long after we met. It was taken that year. Now the old couple are his grandparents, then there are his father, his aunt Gloria and his young uncle Giovanni. Rosa, Raff's mother, is kneeling on the right, Raff is next to her in sun-glasses, and the little boy is Giovanni and Mona's son. Mona wasn't there to be snapped. But the little boy must be…..'

'Emilio!' cried Melyssa, seizing the frame. 'It would fit! He's nearly forty now, so in '93 he'd have been nine or ten.'

'You've known this photo since you were a little girl,' said Mrs Mosengo. 'It's always been on that shelf. The colour is fading a bit now.'

'Yes, yes, of course, but….'

How could she explain that, although she had noticed the old photo many times, until now she had never looked at the group in it with interest. But now she knew! Her father! And that little boy – Emilio! – and she could see how his man's face had grown from the child's.

Melyssa held the picture a few inches from her face in the clear light. Emilio here! He always had been here. She stopped herself in time from kissing the serious little boy's face.

Then she began to realise that she knew the setting behind the group. The heavy steps, the black stones at the base of *Il Torre del Purgatorio*! She felt a series of shocks: her father, her nightmare place, the man she loved: all here! All had been here. Perhaps that's why I had my dreams about the Black Tower; I'd always, subconsciously, known it.

'You won't ever throw this away, will you Mum?'

'Now when have I ever thrown anything way, Melly? You know what I'm like.' She took the frame from Melyssa's hand. 'I'll put it back where it belongs.'

It was with misgivings that Melyssa caught the bus to Seerwood Avenue. Abraham had the car at work, and Rebecca, whether she drove or not these days, hadn't, in any case, suggested collecting her. Part of her recoiled from the familiar Bristol land marks; they seemed so much part of a childhood she had wanted to forget and from which she had moved on. Another part of her relished them as something stable in a world which was distancing herself from reality. Whatever reality is.

Melyssa felt cold and weak as she slumped in the jiggling seat.

Because the sun was shining, she had decided to wear a loose shirt over her denims, but it seemed chilly. What a failure I am – a failure in love and a failure in business. This phrase pleased her strangely and she found herself mouthing it to the rhythm of the bus. So much for trying to be sophisticated. One setback and I'm back at mummy's. Why couldn't I have stayed on and coped? Her answer came at once: everyone needs a bedrock of trust and love to underpin coping.

'He let me down,' she muttered. 'He made me love him and then he threw me away.' Don't be so melodramatic, you burk. "Threw me away" indeed! *You* walked out on him. I did the throwing away. I walked away from the best contract that Calypso could hope to be awarded, and it will probably scupper the business. We could be sued. At that reflection, Melyssa felt herself go hot and cold. By the time had reached her stop, she was in a state of alarm and fury with herself.

Seerwood Avenue. Dear God. It's exactly like Orchard Road. How many times have I visited Rebecca after school at that neat house halfway down Orchard Road? And this was Rebecca's adult home. A bus-trip away and identical to the house she grew up in. How can she bear it?

Melyssa rang the bell. There was a bustling in the hall. Rebecca, her sharp, lively face expressing welcome, threw open the door. She was wearing a green track suit.

'Mel! Great! Come in, come in. Your mum rang me to say you were back home for a bit. Shut UP, Joseph,' she added, as her chubby, bright-eyed son came rushing down the hall imitating a fire-engine. 'This is my friend, Melyssa. She having her lunch with us, so you've got to be a good boy. Say hello.'

Joseph put out his plump arms and gave Melyssa a warm kiss as she bent down to greet him. She clumsily responded. She knew that she had never been very good with small kids; when she had taught Art and Design it had been at a secondary school and her favourite pupils had been GCSE and A Level candidates between fifteen and eighteen. Noisy, demanding toddler brats were really not her scene, she told herself.

'I've got three tractors. Do you want to see them?'

'Oh, um. Super. Later though. Later I'd – I'd love to,' replied Melyssa, not able to inject much enthusiasm into her voice, for she had little fondness for tractors, full-size or toy.

'Bonny should be back in a few minutes,' said Rebecca. 'She's been round with her friend. Do you want to give me a hand in the kitchen?'

Melyssa followed her into the neat kitchen. There was a nice smell coming from the oven.

'I hope you're hungry, Mel.'

'*I'm* hungry,' shouted Joseph, slipping his warm hand into Melyssa's long, chilly one. She was about to pull her hand away when, to her surprise, she found she liked the feel of the boy's confident grip. She summoned a grin.

'I could eat a whole horse,' she said to him. How lucky, she thought, that I had a small breakfast after all.

'You don't eat *horses*!' squealed Joseph, in delight at his ready knowledge. 'You eat pigs and cows and chickens, but not horses!'

'Well, I could eat a whole pig then – if it was a small one,' smiled Melyssa.

'We're having a little part of a pig, and you'll have to leave some for me and Mummy and Bonny, and some for Dad when it's cold.'

'Roast pork,' said Rebecca. 'Okay? Now, Joseph, shut up and let Melyssa's hand go. And go and wash yours, and while you're at it, put away those lorries on the landing before someone skids on one and breaks their neck.'

'I hadn't realised he was so old,' said Melyssa when Joseph had gone upstairs. 'And I've never seen Bonny.'

'Well, you're always in London and, well,' said Rebecca, lowering her voice, 'your interests and mine are so different. I felt we'd grown apart. Not that I mean you'd got a bit stand-offish, but you seemed less keen on keeping up....'

'Oh, Rebecca, if you mean the last time we met, I....'

Melyssa stopped and looked at her old school friend, Rebecca was not a striking girl, but she was pleasant-featured and competent-looking. And she was not unintelligent, and she was kind in a sincere, no-nonsense way. Had she and I grown too far apart, thought Melyssa, to be comfortable with each other?

As if designed to arrest any attempt from either of them to clothe their thoughts in words, the doorbell rang and Rebecca opened the front door to another woman of about her and Melyssa's age. She had two small girls with her.

'Bonny,' said the newcomer, pushing the smaller of the two children into the hall.

'Hello, darling,' smiled Rebecca, bending to kiss Bonny's cheek. 'Oh, this is my friend, Belinda, Mel.'

Belinda came forward into the hall.

'Pleased to meet you,' she said.

'How do you do?' replied Melyssa.

'So she calls you Mel? She calls me Bel,' said Belinda. 'Bel and Mel. What a duo! Still it's better than Ant and Dec. Yet she won't be called Becks.'

'Sounds like what they call a stream up in Yorkshire, or wherever,' riposted Rebecca.

Bonny climbed the stairs to find her brother and Melyssa was left in the hall to hear an animated conversation between Rebecca and her friend, the talkative Belinda.

Forgetful of Melyssa's existence, they swopped stories of nursery school, of toys, of meals tried and meals rejected by their respective broods. At one point they clung together in laughter at some story about what Daniel did in Mrs Laing's lesson. Melyssa, unable to make any sort of response at all, stood next to them, gazing from one to the other. She had to admit that they did seem carefree, happy and fulfilled. And they spoke a different language. Melyssa toyed with the idea of telling them about her dinner-party conversation with Sir Ambrose about the state of Italian opera, but had the sense to see how absurd and inappropriate it would be.

At length Belinda announced that she had to get back.

'Nice to have met you,' she said to the silent Melyssa. 'Sorry to have gone on a bit. But you know how it is. How many have you got?'

'I'm not married, or – or partnered,' said Melyssa. 'So none.'

'Oh,' said Belinda.

'Melyssa's an interior designer in London. She's been working on a theatre in Italy,' said Rebecca.

'Oh,' repeated Belinda, rather obviously dismissing this childless, unmarried person who decorated theatres. 'Fancy that. Well, nice meeting you.'

After a further short storm of conversation, the front door closed on Belinda and her infant.

'She's a one,' said Rebecca approvingly.

After lunch, during which the demands of Joseph and Bonny kept both of them busy, Rebecca and Melyssa gathered up the children's bicycles which filled the space in the cupboard under the stairs, and went out with them to the park. As they whizzed off, squealing, over the grass, their plump legs pushing at the pedals – Bonny on her tiny trike and Joseph on two wheels with out-riders – Rebecca turned to Melyssa and said,

'Let's sit down. We can keep an eye on them from this bench. I haven't had a chance to ask yet, and I don't know if I should, but your mother said you were rather down in the dumps and needed cheering up. So I wondered what the trouble was, and whether I could help.'

Rebecca seemed to hurry this short speech along as if fearful that Melyssa would freeze her out or pretend not to know what she was talking about. Rebecca had not forgotten Melyssa's snub the last time they had met by chance earlier in the summer at Temple Meads station.

'You see, she continued, hurrying on, 'I want to cheer you up if I can, although I don't know much about design and opera and all that. I asked your mum if it was a health issue and I was so relieved to hear that it wasn't, but she told me you'd come back unexpectedly, so I realised that something had gone phut with the job. I mean,' she added, 'I knew it wouldn't be anything to do with a man.'

Because that last bleak sentence told her so much of what people thought about her, Melyssa fell into a grim silence as Rebecca's kind, soft voice twittered on.

'Why don't you tell me what's gone wrong? We used to be such friends. Even if I can't do much, it sometimes helps just to talk to someone who isn't involved. And what I can do, I will. I mean, you're welcome to stay here with me if things are a bit sticky at home. We have a spare room.'

It was on the tip of Melyssa's tongue to tell Rebecca where she could stick her offer, but in a sudden shift of understanding, she saw Rebecca as she really was. Happy, generous, kind, busy, pre-occupied with the demands of her kids, but then she did have them to be pre-occupied with. She had a cosy home full of the objects of shared love and hope. She had a man who came back from work to her arms. She had those children and, although Melyssa knew from her mother that she'd had to give up work while Bonny was too young for school, and couldn't afford full-time nursery care, yet that sacrifice would pass and she would soon be bound up in their exciting futures.

The future. What future did Melyssa look forward to?

What could Melyssa say she had? Driven by ambition, by the demands of changing design fads, of on-line expectations and branding concerns and wanting to be oh-so-different from people like Rebecca, she had just ended up with what? A half-share in a small shop in South London, the business of which was handled in the main by her young brother. And then she had gone abroad and become infatuated, like a schoolgirl or someone in a film, with the first glamorous man she had met. Withdrawn, hard, touchy, loveless, cut off from friends and family, interested only in a fashionable and costly world to which she did not belong: this was her life. She had nothing. By comparison Rebecca was enormously rich.

As these reflections chased across her tired mind, two tears welled up and ran down her cheeks.

Rebecca, who had been looking across to where Joseph and Bonny were making overtures to some other children by the trees, turned back to Melyssa and gasped in alarm at the sight of those tears.

'Oh, Melly, there is something *very* wrong, isn't there?'

Impulsively she took Melyssa's hand in hers and held it tight. 'I'm your friend, then and now, you know.'

Melyssa's voice came out harshly, although she did not take her hand away, as she replied,

'First of all there *is* a man. Or rather there was. I was – am – in love for the first time. Nothing else matters except the pain of not being with him. Can you know what I mean?'

'Of course I can. Of course I know. I felt just the same before we were engaged.'

Melyssa smothered the feeling of disbelief that anyone else could have felt as she did – and over a man as ordinary as Rebecca's husband. And yet, she thought, love was love. Astonishing to think it, but Rebecca had probably gone through the same agonised longings, the same physical excitements, doubts, temptations that she had done. It was what, perhaps, they had in common. She held Rebecca's hand more tightly as she continued,

'I think you are so lucky, Rebecca. You have everything in the world. I wanted, I admit, to be different from you and all the people round here. I needed so desperately to get away from Mum, from the school, from

Bristol, and to try to *be* someone. I thought I was getting there in London. And when Calypso landed the job in Italy, I really felt I'd broken through. Oh, I wish you could have seen me at the villa, with the Carrara mountains behind and the sea at Via Reggio in front, on the warm marble terrace in the morning with Emilio. There were days when I could hardly believe it was me.'

'Emilio is the man, eh?' said Marjorie. 'Dear Mel, you always liked Italians.'

'Yes, as you reminded me at the station before I left. Poor Angelo. I wanted so much more to come of that, you know. But his mother kept an eye on us both. He told me once that she believed he had a vocation to the Catholic priesthood. Emilio is, I guess, a ready-made perfect model of what Angelo might have been. And that's not the only reason, Rebecca, why I find myself yearning for him. He's older than I am, and with a Mediterranean skin and those romantic good looks – you know – but what may tip the scales is that I have discovered, Rebecca, that I am half-Italian myself.'

Rebecca gaped at her.

'You! How *can* you be?'

'Since I saw you last I've discovered that my dad isn't my dad, that T-ray is my half-brother and my mum had a passionate relationship with an Italian Bristol uni student. I was born, and then he died of a rare form of blood cancer. Mum married dad when I was only a few months old. I never knew my real father, obviously, but his genes are in me, so….'

'Well!' gasped Rebecca. 'What a story! So dramatic. And so interesting. Do I gather then that this Emilio, the man you love, is responsible for the Italian project you're on?'

'Yes. He did a Sherlock Holmes and hunted me down to Calypso Designs in Battersea. And why, you ask? Because my real father was a sort of second-cousin of his. So we are distantly related. He wants to build a school for young singers with a theatre attached in a small Tuscan hilltop town. He is, as a matter of fact, Emilio Monza.'

Melyssa paused in expectation of an exclamation of recognition from Rebecca, feeling, too late, like someone name-dropping, and hoping Rebecca wouldn't find it crass and boastful of her. But she needn't have worried. Rebecca wrinkled her placid brow.

'I don't think I've heard of him,' she said at last. 'Should I have?'

At that, Melyssa felt a great spurt of laughter welling up inside her. It was topped by affection for her old friend. Grabbing Rebecca's hand, she laughed until the park dissolved in sparkles in front of her eyes.

'Oh Rebecca!' she cried, as her friend stared in alarm at her. 'You've made me sane again! Of course you shouldn't have heard of him.'

Joseph and Bonny, dropping their little bikes, came running up in amazement. Joseph looked at Melyssa and said,

'You're like the clown at the circus.'

'Yes, Joseph. I am a clown. Hey, let me get us all some ice-creams.'

A little later, having kissed Rebecca and felt warmer and more at one with her than at any time since their school days, Melyssa left her and walked home through the quiet suburban streets. It was amazing how much better she felt after her healthy afternoon in the park with her old pal and the romping kids. She was so filled with warmth towards Rebecca and the happy, fulfilled life she led, that part of her mind toyed with moving back to Bristol. It's where I started, she thought, and may be where I belong. The design shop, the project in Italy, her infatuation with Emilio; all now seemed ridiculously unreal and oddly distant.

Getting close to home, she saw, with a shock, the Calypso Designs van parked outside.

She ran up to the front door and was about to put her key in the lock when the door opened. T-ray stood before her. His eyes snapped at her, his lips were compressed.

'So,' he said, in a loud, unnatural voice.

What's this? thought Melyssa. What wrong with him?

'So, you have come back from your walk, have you?'

Why, he's almost like an unfriendly stranger, thought Melyssa as she came tentatively into the house. Or – or is he still unwell?

T-ray slammed the door shut.

'You damned, unreliable little...,' he began, but Melyssa interrupted him, crying,

'T-ray! Oh T-ray, I wanted to see you and tell you why I can't do that job. That project in Italy. You see I....'

'Shut up, you useless idiot!' T-ray shouted. Melyssa gazed at him with wide eyes, her face frozen in shock. She backed away from him into the sitting-room, the crooks of her knees caught the edge of the sofa, and she slumped down on it, open-mouthed.

'I nearly had a stroke when mum rang and told me what you'd done,' T-ray continued, biting off the words rather than uttering them. 'Just what the hell came over you? You walk out in the middle of a contract, you fly back to the UK without a word to Signor Monza, you swan back home here as if you had nothing particular to do at the moment. Is this your idea of professional business? Is this the way to get Calypso Designs known and respected? We've both worked our butts off up to now to get the firm going; you're entrusted with the most important contract we've ever had, and you just ponce about and walk out in the middle of it. Are you totally raving mad?'

He stood over her, really infuriated, his voice coming in a hoarse shout. Melyssa tried to speak.

'You, you don't understand. They ganged up on me – Bertini, the Contessa – and our proposals were criticised, our projections made fun of. But I could have stood all that, if Emilio.... I was in so in love, T-ray, and it seemed hopeless. I just....'

'Love!' hooted T-ray. 'Love! What are you talking about? What the hell does *that* matter? What does your silly love-life matter, you fool? I've heard something about that from Mum. So what? Who cares if you get a crush on the boss? What about the contract? It's the *contract* that matters!'

'But I did try. I did the designs, I made the computer projections, but at the site, they…. Oh, you don't understand,' wailed Melyssa.

'I fucking do understand. We have no penalty clause, but the contractors do. If they get stung for finishing late – and you know, because Emilio told us, that quite a lot of outfits have been persuaded to invest in the project – do you think they're not going to come gunning for us for compensation? I mean, how long were you going to take holidaying down here?'

'Look,' interrupted Melyssa, jumping up as some of her spirits returned, 'you don't realise what was going on out there. You only came over once in a whole month. I was on my own. In the end, I couldn't cope.'

'Well, you shouldn't have gone then, should you?'

'I *told* you I didn't want to go right at the beginning. But you chucked me into it, and then got Covid. Remember?'

'As you obviously can't manage to cope with anything more demanding than selling rolls of wallpaper in the shop, I'll tell you what I've done. I rang Signor Monza and told him where you were. He was worried about you personally. God knows why. And I've offered to go out myself and finish the job. Fortunately he's a decent guy and hasn't told us to stuff our contract. In short, man to man, we sorted it out. God! Why didn't I take you at your word in the first place and leave you out of it?'

At the thought that T-ray had spoken to Emilio, come to a new arrangement without consulting her, and the shame of it all, Melyssa drew in her breath to reply with rage and hurt, but T-ray, with a roughness he had never shown his sister before, shoved her back on the sofa and gave her some more of his mind.

'You are a shallow, impetuous, self-centred, emotionally unbalanced bitch, dear sister of mine; half-sister, I should say. You have, and always have had, a chip on your shoulder about men. You've never had a steady boyfriend like most girls your age. You drive guys away. You're an unreasonable, demanding, obsessive fake. All this broad-shouldered business woman, "I'm better than any man at any job" bollocks has gone to your head. Add to all that your touchiness about being black – and you ain't as black as me, and we now know why – and you've got quite a package. Then one man, the one who has given you the contract of the decade, gets up your "I hate all men, but I want them to admire me" nostrils for some reason or other, and you up and run, like the self-important, selfish silly brat you really are. Typical! There just ain't no point in trusting women with real responsibility, no matter what the PC crowd say. Look at Liz Truss! Useless, and,' he said, running out of steam, 'you're the most useless of the lot!'

After giving her one more scornful look, he left the room.

Melyssa remained on the sofa, unable to move. She knew that somewhere in the house her mother, too frightened, or too tactful to emerge, was hiding away, but had heard every word. T-ray – how could you turn on me like that?

All the calm, regained confidence and sense of proportion which the afternoon with Rebecca had given her had evaporated. Somewhere she heard a door shut. Has he gone? Am I such a fool, such a bitch as he thinks? Everyone despises me. Are they right to do that?

Standing shakily, for the upset of her one-sided interview with T-ray filled her mind, Melyssa looked in the mirror over the fireplace. Her face seemed composed – a poor reflection of what seethed within. With an automatic gesture she smoothed her hair, which looked more of a dark corona than ever, for she had not been to a hairdresser in her weeks in Tuscany, and looked at her bright lipstick to check it hadn't got smudged. Oh, shit, I'm more like a carefully preserved doll than a real person. No one treats me like a human being with feelings. I'm a joke to everyone.

It's so unfair.

She opened the sitting-room door and listened. There seemed to be no one in the house, but she felt sure her mother was lurking somewhere. T-ray appeared to have left, unless he was in the garden. She peeked out of the sitting-room window. Yes, he had left. The Calypso Designs van was no longer parked outside.

Melyssa felt a violent need for privacy and silence. She went quietly upstairs to her room, closed the door and leant against it for a moment. She crossed to the curtains, drew them, and kicked off her jeans and then her shoes. With the afternoon sunlight blushing through the curtains, she climbed into bed and curled into a ball of misery. She remembered last doing this when she had learned that she had failed to get a part in the school play. She pressed her head into her pillow, forgetful of her lipstick and screamed as loudly as she could, muffling the sound as she abandoned herself to the luxury and the pain of hysteria and self-pity. She ground her face into her pillow in a physical rictus which mirrored her inner turmoil. Loveless, childless, directionless, with her brother and most of Italy ranged against her, she longed for one face to smile on her; the one face that, thanks to her stupid hysteria, she would not see again.

BACK

The afternoon had turned to early evening. Melyssa, exhausted by her hysterics and feelings of shame and inadequacy, had passed into sleep. She had not heard voices in the hall of the house beneath her.

She slept still as the handle of the bedroom door turned. Light through the curtains fell on her face. Her lovely profile was shaded. Her long, curled lashes were over her eyes. The tumbled corona of her hair spread over the pillow. Her lips were slightly parted and her fingers gripped the edge of the duvet close under her chin.

A shadowy shape was in the room, gently closing the door again. Melyssa moaned faintly and turned in her sleep. The curve of her cheek was lovely; one of her long legs was revealed by her movement.

The shape approached the bed and lowered itself onto the edge. Melyssa's hand instinctively sought the form next to her and laid itself on an arm.

Emilio Monza sat on the bed of the beautiful girl from Bristol and listened to her breathing. His hand took hers while she slept.

Downstairs Mrs Mosengo was speaking to her son in awed tones.

'He seems really nice. You'd never think he was such a famous man. Fancy him coming here – being here. And so worried about Melly.'

'Hm,' grunted T-ray, who had not gone back to London, but had taken the van to do a bit of shopping for his mother after his angry talk to his sister. 'I think it's unbelievably decent of him. I was gob-smacked to hear that he'd grabbed the first plane out of Pisa. He must be soft on her – amazing though that may seem. He needs to get to SpecSavers.'

'Typical of a brother,' smiled Mrs Mosengo. 'Your sister is a very beautiful girl.'

'Yes, well, in a chilly warrior-princess sort of way, perhaps,' admitted T-ray. 'But I don't get the half of it. She rushes away in mid-job, but instead of being peeved, he comes racing across Europe to see how she is. Still,' he continued with a warm ring to his voice, 'I'm no end relieved.

I really went for Mel when I thought she'd blown the contract. Perhaps I was a bit hard on her. I don't know.'

'You were a bit, from what I could hear. You were yelling at her at one point. Poor little Melly.'

'If she's had a rough time over in Tuscany, I can take that in; but I still think walking out on the project was going too far.'

'He's nothing like I thought he'd be,' said Mrs Mosengo, changing the subject, 'he's very charming and sort of ordinary, in a rather sweet way. I can't get over that he is related to Mel's father, poor Raffaello. And you wouldn't think he was a multi-millionaire. He dresses like anyone else, doesn't he?'

'So do Elon Musk, Prince Harry and Ed Sheeran, to name but three. You didn't expect him to turn up in a dress-suit and a top-hat, did you?'

'No, of course not, you twit. But you did say he was worldly-wise and rather off-hand and full of himself when you first met him, T-ray.'

'I thought he was. But clearly he feels differently about Sleeping Beauty upstairs, thank God. I really was expecting a row and a bill for walking out on a contract, thanks to her.'

'I'll get dinner going as he's staying for it, Thanks for getting those chicken breasts,' said Mrs Mosengo. 'I'm doing them West Indian style. I hope he likes them. Your dad certainly does, and he'll be home any minute. Look, he's having your old room, T-ray. I'm not letting him go to a hotel tonight. You can stay down the road with Joan Tulliver. I don't suppose you want to drive back to London later.'

'No. I want to stay and help sort out the mess. Hope those two up there are making up.'

'So, Melyssa,' said Emilio, still holding her warm fingers in his. 'I had an idea where you had gone and why, even before T-ray contacted me. I was shocked to realise how unhappy you had been that you should do such a thing. Why didn't you come to me?'

Melyssa, astonished on awakening to find Emilio in her bedroom, and still overwhelmed by the joy and alarm of it, could find nothing to say.

'Why did you not tell me how badly the job was getting you down? Bertini is not a hard man, but like many Italians he is not used to working with a woman, let alone a woman of colour, let alone under her directions. Bertini still lives in the 1980s. He was bound to snipe at everything you suggested. It would have been a matter of male pride and of European superiority of race. Surely you've come across his type of man before?'

'No,' replied Melyssa, finding her voice at last and struggling into an upright position in the bed. 'I haven't. Not on any job I've tackled in England, at any rate. I don't think anyone here finds it odd that a woman should be a designer, an artist, or thinks that she couldn't possibly be IT and computer-literate. On the contrary. And as for being a POC, as it's called, it hasn't harmed Rishi Sunak, the woman who headed up John Lewis, the leader of the SNP and Welsh Labour, and plenty more. We are a quarter way through the twenty-first century, for God's sake.'

She wondered as she spoke if she should put on the bedside light, but was not sure if she looked puffy, blotchy and dishevelled after her recent fits and sleep. She decided to remain softly lit by the summer evening glow from the curtained window.

'But to hell with Bertini,' she went on, 'what on earth are you doing here? I mean, I realise how you got here, but – but why?'

Melyssa found to her surprise that she was able to speak with spirit. She knew that she had been close to some sort of mental breakdown; had known on her surreal flight back to her beginnings – but her sleep, and the presence of Emilio in her room, put heart back into her, so that she was able to respond rationally to him.

'Why?' smiled Emilio. 'Why did I come here? Why do you think?'

'Is – is it because you don't want to change project designers in mid-contract?'

'Yes, of course I don't,' replied Emilio seriously. He applied a little pressure on her hand and shifted a little closer to her on the bed. 'But there is so much more. I was so very worried when they told me you had checked out of the *pensione*. I was worried when you checked *into* it, for that matter. I was so sure you felt as I did, and then it seemed you didn't.'

'Felt what? You're not talking about the theatre, are you?'

'No, I am not! You must have known what an impact you made on me from the moment we met. Surely you must know what a strikingly lovely woman you are. I wanted to put business in the way of Raffaello's child, of course, and that's why I found out where you were, but the work on the project was only ever part of it. When you swam out to the yacht and let me look after you, I realised that you were going to mean something very, very special to me. And then you grew distant and withdrawn. I couldn't imagine why, but I began to see a reason. You were envious. We Italians know all about envy.'

'I *was* envious! Of course I was,' cried Melyssa, and then she lowered her voice again as it occurred to her that her mother might hear every word. 'Of course I was envious,' she hissed, 'envious of Loredana, jealous of her – and what you and she had between you.'

Even as she spoke, Melyssa was aware that Emilio was looking surprised. It seemed that he hadn't expected her to say that.

'Of Loredana and me?' he re-iterated. 'Do you mean love? There is nothing between us in that line.'

'But, but....'

'I thought you were envious of my wealth and were resentful of my assumption of leadership and control of the project's designs. I thought you would resent a rich European man lording it over a working girl.'

'There was – is, something between you. I'm sure of that. She acts as though she owns you, and when she spoke to me it was as a competitor in love. I felt it from the beginning.'

He was silent. He seemed to be hunting for the right words. Melyssa watched him closely. This was awful really. He had travelled so far to be with her, and she was putting him on the spot. But she knew that this had to be cleared up. Either he loved her – and her heart rejoiced at that stupendous prospect – or he loved Loredana. The ambiguities she had sensed in the Contessa's relationship with him had to be explained.

'Hm, yes,' Emilio said at last. 'A woman's instinct is never wrong. Long ago, and I do mean long ago, Melyssa, there was a time when… But it was never love. I was ashamed of what I had done. Loredana's late husband was my aunt's son, and we were friendly. He was only six years older than I was, but he had a title and had inherited a fortune from his father Count Alberto. He helped me a lot in my early days. But he was dead, killed in the plane crash, before Loredana and I had a brief fling. And it was more on her side than mine. *Dio mio,* "fling" is the wrong word. It was just once. She was widowed, lonely, unhappy, and could not bear living alone in the house in Florence. She stayed in the villa, and one night…… She wasn't always as bitter as she must seem to you now. I think I was sorry for her. It had been such a tragedy. And she used to be attractive, and her helplessness made an impression on me. So you see…'

Emilio's voice tailed away. Melyssa gazed at his sad face. Yes, now she came to think of it, he did have a sad face, especially in repose and away from the public eye. Yet one more thing had to be cleared up. She hardened her heart and began to quiz him once more.

'When I was staying at the villa, you and she…. I mean, you were always going to her room. I'm sorry, Emilio, it sounds like spying, but I did see it on several occasions. It was that, more than any woman's instinct, that led me to think that you were lovers.'

'You can only have seen it twice, Melyssa. Twice was all there was. I had to see her. It was about business, well, property and a will. We had to discuss something which would have made a huge difference to my plans. Either you believe me, or you don't. But I'm telling the truth. And I must say,' he continued warmly, 'you were making a lot of assumptions on those two occasions.'

'What else could I have assumed? You didn't look or sound like someone meeting up to discuss business. And I thought you made it pretty clear to me where you were going – and so did she.'

'Yes, yes, I was silly to have done that. I think that I was hoping to jolt you into taking more notice of me. She was just being annoying because she knew you'd be upset. But since that time on the yacht you have shown me no interest, as a woman does for a man. Oh yes, you have talked of carpets and lights and cornices and exit signs, but you have been icy at the same time. I admit it; you have dynamited your way into my life. I can think of nothing but you and your loveliness. But you took no notice of me. It may be boastful to say so, but girls normally *do* take notice of me. You were the fascinating exception. I might have been Scarpia to your Tosca – and what I wanted, what I want now, is to be your Cavaradossi.'

Melyssa, though fond of operatic melodies – on CD, BBC 4, or listening to Classic FM's hit arias – did not understand the full import of these references, but she saw where Emilio was leading. Her heart leapt. Her hand, still imprisoned in his, answered to the pressure of his grip. Her eyes met his in the rosy glow of the bedroom. She wanted very much to say the right thing now. Now, when, at all costs, she must not come over as the detached, professional woman, as Tosca to his Scarpia, whatever that meant, nor must she say anything foolish. She was only too aware how many times she must have come over as an inexperienced, clumsy idiot in his eyes. A shrewd strain in her recognised that, Italian male as he was, Emilio would not hold that against her. He may have criticised Bertini for feeling superior to a woman, but she sensed that, deep down, it was how he looked at things too. No. No, it was not a foolish response she had to avoid making, but a cutting, dismissive one. Had he not rushed to seek her out? A rebuff would do more than just wound him. It might be the final thing that drove him from her.

Her heart burned to know one thing more. She knew that she had not been wrong in seeing jealousy in the Contessa's manner towards her. Jealously, yes, and that something more – a sense that she and Loredana were locked in combat. This had to explained. She hated to think that Emilio could lie to her. But he was a great man: talented, rich, powerful, adored and used to getting his own way in everything. She was nothing. To think that he could coolly use her filled her with a physical horror.

She stared at his dim face.

His integrity meant more to her than anything else at that moment.

'Well, my lovely girl,' came his voice, cutting across her thoughts, 'which am I to be: Cavaradossi or Scarpia?'

'Who was Scarpia?' asked Melyssa, to play for time while she considered how to frame her last question to him – what was that special "business" he had with the Contessa which needed him to see her late at night?

'Scarpia? He was a wicked police chief who fell violently in love with a girl who rejected him. So he set about getting his own way with her. He arrested and tortured the man she loved as a means of getting her to sleep with him. But she remained true to Cavaradossi because she was one of the greatest heroines in Grand Opera. I have played Cavaradossi many times.'

'Have you never played Scarpia?' she whispered.

'I cannot,' he replied. 'It's not physically possible. Scarpia is a bass part and I am a tenor.'

Beneath the allusions was a hardness in his tone that Melyssa did not miss. And she knew of what he was thinking. How free was she?

'I have no lover,' she said clearly. 'There is no one here in the UK. There never has been.'

The relief in his eyes told her a great deal. The internationally famous tenor would have been mortally humiliated had he learned that he was a rival in love to some Bristol estate agent.

Seeing that relief, Melyssa felt that she too was entitled to be freed from the doubts she still entertained about Loredana.

'Did Cavaradossi love anyone other than Tosca?' she asked.

'Ah,' said Emilio, letting go her hand and sitting up straight on the bed's edge. He had come into the room with his sunglasses pushed up on top of his head. He now took them off, folded them and slipped them into his shirt pocket. 'So we're back to this? Have I not said? Why should you think I would lie to you?'

'I don't think that at all, yet,' cried Melyssa. 'I'm sorry, Emilio, I know you think me stupid, but I must know what business you and Loredana have and why it makes her hate me, if it isn't competition for your love.'

Emilio stood up.

'She is a clever girl,' he muttered to himself.

Melyssa was not sure whether he was referring to herself or to her supposed rival. He stood silent for a long minute. Downstairs came to clunk of the front door and a jovial call. Abraham Mosengo was back from work. There were voices in the hall, two explaining, one full of surprise. Melyssa could imagine Abraham's astonishment on discovering that he had a famous opera star in the house, staying to dinner, spending the night in his son's old room, and currently closeted with his daughter upstairs in her bedroom. She prayed that he would not play the part of dutiful, protective father and clump upstairs to see what the hell was going on.

There a further sound of a door shutting, then quiet. No danger from Dad then, thought Melyssa with deep gratitude.

'You are too perceptive for me to treat you as I am doing,' said Emilio at last. 'You sense what is behind the obvious and by instinct take the right action. If you had not come home to Bristol and brought me into your mother's orbit, I should probably not have revealed what I am now going to tell you.'

Good heavens, thought Melyssa. What on earth is coming now?

'I would have told you eventually – although I am not sure when. It is only fair that you should know. But I would probably just let you have your share in the profits of the theatre while it got established, if any, as a sort of retainer fee for your design company's continuing supervision of the site and further projects on it.'

The words ran over Melyssa's head. She shook her bush of black hair in puzzlement.

'I don't understand.'

'Look, look. Loredana's husband, Count Dominico, owned a huge swathe of land on and around the hills of Borgo San Martino. But, he didn't own the Black Tower, *Il Torre del Purgatorio*, and its associated *palazzo* and approach. That was owned by Cinthio D'Andrea, left to him by *his* father. He in turn left it to his eldest son, Frederico, born in 1949. My father, born in 1952, was the youngest of the three, so he couldn't have it. His daughter, Gloria, Dominico's mother, was a woman. No Tuscan of Cinthio's day, born a hundred years ago, leaves land or property to a woman. Frederico then naturally left it to *his* son, Raffaello. Upon Raffaello's death it goes on to his child – his grandson, the old man hoped. He too assumed a boy, of course, would look after it.'

'What grandson?'

'No grandson. A grand-*daughter*, and she is….'

'What are you saying?'

'His grand-child is you, Melyssa. *Il Torre del Purgatorio* belongs to you.'

'The tower is mine?' she gasped.

The Black Tower, the theatre now part of it, the school – all is yours now. And I say "now" because I have been busy with lawyers in Italy ever since I found you. It took a bit of doing, I must say. There was no record of your birth in Italy and Raffaello had left no will. It was a fine legal matter of natural succession. Luckily today, women's interests are protected, even in Italy. Of course, by that time I had given birth to my great idea.'

'The school for poor young singers?'

'And the theatre. A start and some hope for boys and girls like myself. And a fine Tuscan performance venue. A dream that could not be sacrificed.'

'Why did you think it might be sacrificed?'

'How was I to know that a young girl from Britain would want what I wanted? You might have wished to sell it off, or build holiday houses on it. So, rather than that, I decided to tell you nothing until it was too late. It was wrong of me, I know. But it's why I hunted down Calypso Designs to do work on the project. I – I suppose it was a sop to a guilty conscience.'

'But I think it is a wonderful idea!'

'Yes, I know. You said that the moment I explained in London. And that helped me very much. I knew we were soul-mates on that at least. Melyssa, it's why I am here now; why I came after you. The Black Tower project is *your* project. You see that now? It's why you can't turn your back on it.'

Melyssa did see it, when it was put like that. A feeling of pride and commitment rose in her. After all, it was rather marvellous to be at the heart of such a grand design, yet not have to worry about paying for it all, because Emilio and his backers were doing that.

'But Loredana?' asked Melyssa. 'How does it affect her?'

'Her late husband, Count Dominico, had no interest in a ruin on a hill, but Loredana, who inherits his property has a considerable interest – and it's not theatrical or educational. So – to answer your final question: it is of your power as a beneficiary under a will, dear Melyssa, that Loredana is jealous and angry; not as a rival to my love. You have no rival, my sweet girl. I've loved you from the beginning. Do you see now?'

Melyssa nodded, her mind and heart light and singing. She pulled at his hand and brought him close to her.

'Let me kiss you,' she whispered. 'Just that. As a sign that I am yours, and you are mine, always. That is true, isn't it?' He nodded.

Their lips came together and his arm slipped round her shoulders. Their embrace was tender and gentle, with no touch of the fierce, disturbing desire of the time on the yacht. Melyssa thought: this is love, not just sex. I do believe him and I do adore him. Such happiness!

They sat, him on the bed's edge, she in it, and let each other's eyes search their faces. Only a minute passed, but it seemed a long time to both of them. At last Emilio, clearing his throat – for he had been close to tears in his joy – said,

'But look, what I have to tell you next ought to be heard by your mother and step-father and T-ray. Let's go downstairs and join them.'

Melyssa nodded again.

'You go on,' she said, 'and tell them I'm coming. I need to get my trousers on when I get out of bed, and doll up a bit before I'm seen in bright light.'

'You look as lovely as ever, if I can say so,' grinned Emilio. 'Trousers or no trousers, lipstick or no lipstick, hair-brush or no hair-brush.'

'Oh, you!' laughed Melyssa, all trace of her sorrows gone.

Abraham Mosengo had been surprised to learn that a well-known singer was upstairs in his daughter's bedroom, but when Yolanda and T-ray had explained he took a chilled lager from the fridge and sat down to look at Channel 4 News.

Soon supper was ready and Mrs Mosengo was about to call up when Emilio appeared on the stairs. She noticed that he looked happy but also a little wary, as though wondering what his presence and further news would mean to the family.

'Signor Monza,' said Mrs Mosengo, 'please come into the dining-room. I hope Caribbean chicken with sweet potatoes and salad will be okay for your supper. It's what I was going to make for us today.'

'Signora Mosengo, it sounds delicious,' smiled Emilio. 'I'm grateful and so pleased to be with you all.'

Abraham, hearing his voice, came out and introduced himself.

'You are the bearer of remarkable things,' he said. 'What one might call the long arm of Italy stretching from the past to today. I think it right that Melyssa knows now about her real dead father. She is such a lovely child, but rather prone to speculation and worry.'

'I must tell you, Signor Mosengo, that I have conceived very warm feelings for Melyssa, and I believe they are returned.'

'That makes you even more welcome, Signor Monza. You have given T-ray's and Melyssa's design firm enormous opportunities.'

Melyssa came down, her hair, make-up and clothing all perfect. Emilio gazed at her with love and admiration.

'Got over your heebie-jeebies?' asked her irreverent brother.

Melyssa smiled at them all, and took a chair next to Emilio.

After supper, and a bottle of white wine, the family and their guest settled down in the sitting-room to hear Emilio's further comments about the theatre at Borgo and the difficulties that faced the project.

'I'm going to start by telling you more about Contessa Loredana. I know, T-ray, that you got on well with her when you met in London. And I know, Melyssa, that you began to dislike her more and more when in Italy. Now I need to tell you both, and your parents, what is at stake. Loredana has wanted, ever since her husband's death, to sell all the agricultural property he owned. The land is worth a lot and it produces fine olive oil and wines, among other crops. She has never valued these things; she's a town girl really, and she needs the sales to top up money. In her widowhood she has run through huge amounts of what Dominico left on holidays, dresses, living it up, and…'

'Drink,' put in Melyssa.

'Yes. You're right. She is an alcoholic, I'm afraid.'

'But does what she wants to sell affect the Black Tower Project?' asked

T-ray. 'Nothing grows on that hill.'

'Now we come to the latest facts,' responded Emilio. 'What do you know about green energy in Italy?'

The Mosengos, T-ray and Melyssa looked blank.

'You mean wind-farms, solar energy, wave-generation?' asked Abraham. 'Here, near the River Severn, we are strongly involved. The tide there runs highest in Britain and there are plants to harness the water rushing in. But Italy? No, one doesn't hear much about green eco-plans over there on British news.'

'Windfarms in Italy are mainly in the south. There are over sixteen hundred plants in Puglia and twelve hundred in Campania. They generate a sixth of Italy's energy, which isn't much compared to a lot of other EU countries. In Tuscany there are only one hundred and forty-four plants, but it has been decided that Tuscany will have five hundred in only five or six years' time.'

'Sorry, Emilio,' put in T-ray. 'this is of interest, of course, but does the plan affect your great idea?'

'Yes, it does. You need to consider the geography of the Arno. After Florence it flows directly west via Pisa into the Tyrrhenian sea – not far from Monte Bulciano and my villa, in fact. Melyssa, you must have noticed a feature of the Arno valley, and indeed the areas on each side of it each day in mid-summer.'

'Um, you mean the heat?' ventured Melyssa.

'Yes, the heat, made more trying by....?'

'Oh! By that really hot wind, the *scirocco*, isn't it?'

'It is indeed. That maddening westerly wind that blows almost all day. And, in the winter, not that you've been there then, in what direction does the wind generally come from, as low pressure systems are carried across Europe?'

'The west. I see what you are getting at,' said T-ray. Abraham and Mrs Mosengo sat fascinated by this information. Emilio had everything at his fingertips. Melyssa could now see vaguely where this information was heading.

'And Loredana sees what you're getting at too,' she mused.

'She does. She wants wind-turbines on her dead husband's land and in particular, up on the hills around Borgo San Martino. In fact, to be even more particular, on the site of the old *palazzo* and the Black Tower. She doesn't want to see the establishment of a school, a centre for the performing arts and a restoration of *Il Torre del Purgatorio.* She wants the whole lot to be demolished and cleared for wind-turbines. She knows what prices are being paid for land to be used for wind-generation. It's all far more appealing to her now she is slowly going bust than a loss-making charity and a theatre that may not make decent money and break even for five years.'

'My God!' cried Melyssa. 'That's why, from the beginning, she told me the plan would never work. And why she's been so anti it since I came out to work with you!'

'Exactly. And now it has been established that the site is legally yours, Melyssa, as Raffaello's child, she's hopping mad and has been trying to counter the inheritance legally. That's why I have had to wrangle with her, often into the night. She got nowhere with the lawyers, but I don't see her quietly giving up.'

'Cripes!' gasped T-ray. 'What wheels within wheels! But you're going so fast. What did you mean just then about Melyssa owning the Black Tower?'

'Just what I was going to ask,' put in Abraham.

'And me,' said Mrs Mosengo. 'Melly owning an Italian building? How on earth could that be possible? Unless – unless it's something to do with poor Raff. Oh, it must be! Please tell us, Signor Monza.'

'Of course. I'm sorry I've sprung it as such a surprise to you. I've remembered that I only told Melyssa when we were alone upstairs earlier this evening. It's true though. Cinthio D'Andrea willed it via his eldest son Frederico to his grandson, Raffaello, Melyssa's father, and to Raffaello's child, whom he assumed, back in the 1950s, would be his great-grandson, a boy. And I hadn't decided to let her know earlier, in case she opposed my plans. I've admitted that to her, haven't I, my darling girl?'

'You have – and, as I said, you needn't worry about any opposition from me. I love and believe in what you are constructing there.'

'But why....?' began T-ray.

'Why didn't I tell you both when I got Calypso Designs on to the job? Well, as I told your sister, getting your firm involved was a sort of salve to my conscience. I think I would have told you soon anyway. But Loredana's position has now made it vital that you know – and you too, Signor and Signora Mosengo.'

He paused and reached for Melyssa's hand, brought it to his lips and kissed it. He looked her in the eyes. She had a sudden insight into what he was going to say to her parents.

'My love, my love,' she whispered.

'I – er – I want everything to be honest and true,' continued Emilio, 'if I am going to be your son-in-law, you know.'

'Oh, darling!' cried Melyssa, leaping up and flinging her arms round his neck.

The Airbus A320 was above the Alps. The stewards of BA had cleared away the remains of the in-flight meal. In first-class seats, Melyssa and Emilio sipped white wine and looked out over the startling white peaks spread out in light and shadow beneath them. Pisa was only forty minutes away and Melyssa was still rotating in her brain the events which had preceded their journey back to London with T-ray.

Emilio had told her that he wanted to marry her! That was the first, the most wonderful, most delirious fact that she had to digest. Then there was the Black Tower – the tower she had so often dreamed about and upon which she had lavished so much time and effort since June – and it was hers! She now had complete faith in his integrity, and had a renewed, but less pressured sense of the exciting responsibility she now had for its final development.

She squeezed his arm and looked at his face, lit by alpine snows.

And there was the impression he had made on her mother; to be charming, but also unaffected and boyish, and so much at ease with Yolanda Mosengo. She thought she could see that, internationally known star as he was, he understood and liked, in women, the simple, the domestic. She knew he had a strong affection for both his dead grandmother Patrizia and his mother, Mona. He had told Melyssa all about her, and had made arrangements to meet so that his *fidanzata* could get to know her. Mona D'Andrea, widowed in 2021, lived now in Florence with an order of nuns. Emilio had said that, in many respects, she resembled Melyssa's mother, and that he loved that.

There is nothing of the spoilt sophisticate about him when you get to know him, thought Melyssa. The arrogant air which he radiated in London at The Dorchester was a kind of protective shellac. When away from crowds and the *paparazzi* he is a different creature, she thought. In fact, when she had been able to see him through her mother's eyes, she had seen her mother differently too. No longer as the slightly faded, mixed-race, provincial woman with a simple little job, a husband for whom she did so much, and a closed horizon – which is how the teenage Melyssa had pigeon-holed Mrs Mosengo and was anxious to leave behind in a Bristol suburb, but as someone fulfilled, kindly and with a fascinating back story; someone entitled to her daughter's respect and love.

Melyssa, not for the first time in her unplanned visit to Bristol, had been made to feel ashamed of her old attitude and determined to change for the better. Her recent standards: the importance of branding, worship of on-line influencers, admiration of money, obsessive self-awareness –

all seemed shallow and pointless. Emilio boasted of his ordinary origin, was building a school for poor children, was doing good with his money. Why should I despise my origins? Perhaps it sounds more romantic to say one is of Tuscan farming stock, rather than admit to being a middle-income ethnic girl from Somerset, but when all is said and done, what's the difference?

The fact that T-ray had, before they went to sleep that night, retracted his words to her, gave her relief. She really hated quarrelling with her brother, now her business partner. Yet she knew that much of what he had told her had been truth. Her frigid, inverted sense of difference and superiority and her lonely ambition had become her prison. How lucky she had been to see her mistakes in time!

The Airbus gave a little dip as if to let Italy know it was arriving. Touch-down at Pisa was now less than half-an-hour away. The air-hostess came to their seats.

'Signor Monza,' she said, 'the Captain sends his compliments and wonders whether you and your companion would like to visit the flight deck.'

Melyssa, not used to flying at the best of times, gasped with pleasure. This was the benefit of travelling with a famous person.

'Good to have you aboard, Sir,' said the Captain – a man named Charles Howard, as Melyssa could see from his gold lapel badge – and he and Emilio shook hands. 'I am a great fan,' went on the Captain. 'I thought you gave the finest performance of Don Giovanni at Covent Garden, before the pandemic in 'nineteen, that I have ever heard.'

'Thank you. Thank you. *Grazie mille,*' murmured Emilio, putting his arm round Melyssa to bring her forward into the ring of breath-taking light from the semi-circle of windows on the flight-deck. She was introduced to Captain Howard. The flight engineer also shook their hands and hung back from Melyssa, smiling and nervous, as if from a celebrity. Over the next ten minutes, until a beep signal came over a loudspeaker on the bulkhead, the Captain pointed out the coastline, the islands and far line of mountains running up Italy's spine to merge into the Alps. He asked Melyssa if she knew that from the flight deck at maximum flying height one could see the Alps as one flew over Paris. Melyssa shook her head wordlessly.

Back in their seats, she clasped Emilio's hand.

'That was wonderful,' she sighed. 'I never thought I'd ever get onto a flight deck. Wasn't the view amazing?'

'Hm. Not as impressive as the Northern polar cap,' replied Emilio, polishing his nails on his lapel in playful schoolboy manner.

'Oh you!' cried Melyssa. 'I might have known you'd done it tons of times already.'

'Well, only once before,' admitted Emilio, grinning. 'Still, once you have done it, you've done it....ow!' He broke off as Melyssa pinched his his wrist. 'It's just that I'm usually in a retinue and I guess they don't want a whole mass of bodies up there. An airline pilot I met in New York told me he'd had Tom Cruise on his flight deck several times. Depends who you are, doesn't it?'

Melyssa snuggled close to him as the Airbus dropped out of the clear sky into the golden misty heat of Pisa.

Sidney was there to meet them beyond customs.

'Hi, sister,' was his greeting. 'Back on the job again? I thought we'd seen the last of you. You were powerful mad a few days ago.'

He seized their luggage and threw it into the back of the Bentley which had met her the first time she had arrived at Galileo Galilei nearly two months ago. On that occasion Loredana had been inside, ready to mix drinks from the car's little bar. Sidney drew a car touch-key from his rumpled white coat.

'There y'are, boss,' he said. 'Have fun.' He jumped into the Bentley and it purred away.

'Right,' said Emilio. 'Let's go.'

'Why aren't we going back with Sidney?' asked Melyssa.

'Because we are not going home yet. Have you forgotten what date it is?'

He led her across to the parking lot beyond the arrivals road, and there was the red Porsche convertible which had clearly been left for him.

'Sidney dropped this over yesterday. I texted him to say I needed it tonight. He's gone to the villa with the luggage, and you and I are free to enjoy ourselves at….. But then you *have* forgotten, haven't you?'

'I'm so sorry, but I think I have,' smiled Melissa, who was puzzling her brain to recall what precise significance this mid-August day should have had.

'Puccini?' smiled Emilio. 'Torre del Lago? Remember?'

And it came back to her. At the outset of her visit this had been planned as a celebration of her labours at Borgo: the best seats for "*Turandot*" at Puccini's birthplace on the lake. More intimate than Verona, less stuffy than Milan, this was one of Italy's great and lesser-known operatic treats.

Emilio eased himself into the car, pushing his sun-glasses down from his hair onto his nose.

'Hop in, darling one,' said he. 'Perfect timing.' He glanced at the watch on his wrist. Melyssa had always been glad that, unlike too many self-made men, Emilio had not purchased a gold Rolex. His slim silver Rotary had much more restraint and taste – and, of course, made him less likely to become a statistic of the recent "Rolex-snatching" crimewaves in European cities that Melyssa had seen reported on TV. 'I expect,' he added, 'you'd like a drink before our early supper. We don't expect "*Turandot*" to start before eight. It's possible they might delay the start until I got there – although I wouldn't guarantee it.'

He gave her one of his open, boyish smiles and started the car. Soon they were whizzing along the tree-lined coast road to Torre del Lago.

Melyssa had one misgiving about the way things had turned out. In being taken straight from the airport to the opera, she felt that she was not properly dressed. Not that it would have mattered if she had been going to sit up in the high circles of seats with the coachloads of tourists, but she knew that Emilio, as a distinguished audience member, would be in a prime spot and that he and she would, no doubt, meet up with the stars of the opera afterwards. Yet she thought it would seem vain and damping to his glee at surprising her if she had insisted upon making the detour to Monte Bulciano for the dress she had in the luggage that had been snatched away by Sidney at Pisa.

But she need not have worried.

'This,' said Emilio, twenty minutes later, 'is La Stella del Lago, a lovely name; the star of the lake. Lovelier in Italian than in English, perhaps. This where we dine, my love. But first you will want to freshen and change, I know.'

Melyssa, immediately struck by the loveliness of the restaurant and *albergo* on the lake, was shown upstairs to a cool, shaded room. There, on the bed, lay a lovely red dress – plainly cut, but so finely dimensioned and of such expensive material she hardly liked to pick it up. It was a starling red – *her* red, as she knew the moment she saw it. Not all reds suited Melyssa's light brown complexion, but this one seemed to bring the room alive with the glitter of flames and passion. Melyssa felt she would look sensational in it and her spirits soared. Next to it was a long box. This is what Emilio had meant by the comment which had puzzled her: "You will want to change".

He knows I will be irresistible in this, she thought, smoothing the material over her thighs. It was strange how, in the last few hours, she had somehow grown used to thinking of how pleasing she might appear to him, how much she might do for him. The realisation that she had, after so long, someone who loved her enough to want to make her his wife gave her a new confidence and tempered that shrill and sensitive edge to her personality which she had come to recognise and deplore.

When the dress was on, Melyssa opened the box. Inside was a heavy silver pendant with matching bracelet – the sort of thing she often wore to good effect. Next to these, wrapped in tissue paper, was a black angora shawl, perfect for throwing over her shoulders as the hot day turned into a Mediterranean night and sea breezes whispered over the lake. By the bed was a pair of delicate, high-heeled shoes.

Who had put these things here? she thought. It must have been Sidney, on Emilio's orders. Emilio must have been very certain that I would come back with him. At the thought of having been read accurately, like a book, something of the old touchy Melyssa returned.

'The cheek!' she snorted. Then, catching sight of herself in the long mirror on the other side of the room, the shawl over her arm, and her hand clutching the jewellery, she had to laugh. If this was cheek, it was the sort of cheek she could grow to like.

At that moment she heard a light tenor voice from below.

'*La donna e mobile....*' it began. Melyssa had to smile as she heard those famous words from *"Rigoletto"*. It was just like Emilio's humour: subtle and clever. She opened the window and looked down.

'Not as fickle as all that...' she began, and then broke off with a gasp of delight.

From the road, the bulk of the restaurant and hotel had prevented her from getting more than a glimpse of the lake. Now, from her room, the majesty of the water, framed by the marble-capped peaks of the Carrara mountains, its placid sheet aflame from the sun, took the breath from her body. The immensity of water, sky and rock seemed to burst into her room, leaving her feeling as though she floated in space and could see the planet rotating beneath her foot-soles.

'Good view, eh?' came Emilio's voice. There, on a broad terrace laid with white-clothed tables, he stood, one foot on the plinth of a marble urn, dressed in a suit of white material, a dazzling figure. He seems to fill those huge spaces, as the sun fills the sky, thought Melyssa. Perhaps that is what star charisma is: the ability to fill space with your presence.

'Do you like your dress?'

'Oh, yes! It's wonderful. It's all – all wonderful. Emilio, my lover, how can I thank you for planning all this?'

'*E niente*, as we say,' smiled Emilio. 'Don't be too long getting tarted up. Our supper is being prepared. Can't you sniff a little *basilico*, a little garlic and oregano in the air? I know it's only six o'clock, bit I hope you can peck something. And we should have the terrace to ourselves.'

Melyssa noticed for the first time that she was starving, for, not feeling like the food on the aircraft, she not taken more than a coffee and a glass of wine on the flight. She breathed deeply. On the air came the scent of seafood, herbs and woodsmoke.

'I'm coming, darling,' she cried, popping her head back in.

To her delight as she moved about, she was aware of her new dress fitting perfectly. She marvelled at how carefully Emilio had done his homework.

That supper on the terrace of *La Stella del Lago* Melyssa was to remember all her life. It was not just the fluffy, saffron-coloured *risotto* of shellfish, nor the savoury, crunchy-skinned *arosto* which followed, nor the salads of different leaves drenched in sweet olive oil and garlic, nor the tangy *ricotta* cheese on its bed of vine leaves, not the wing-cake of dark chocolate, *crema* and coconut ice-cream which wound up the meal for her – Emilio finding room for a slice of water-melon and a few *specialite di Prato*, little almond cakes, with his coffee. It was not just the glorious position, right on the lake's edge, lit by small lamps – for the coming of the Early Tuscan night had the far mountain caps blushing red in the declining sun. With the murmur of water against the pontoons she and Emilio might have been out in a boat of their own. It was not just Emilio's presence, the way in which he handed her lovely things to eat, nor the electric bringing-together of their legs under the table-cloth, not the long glances he gave her from eyes that, to her mind, glowed with a sensual passion. Not any one of these lifted Melyssa out of herself into a world she had not inhabited before, but all together, all at once, they whirled her senses along in anticipation and fulfilment, so that, when an older woman, she could look back on that one night and understand why she had been born.

They spoke, of course, but she couldn't later remember what they had said. She knew, with a certainty that made her draw in her breath with sexual excitement, that later they would make love. That night, hardly yet begun, she received at last the balm for all the anxious questing, yearnings and disappointments of her earlier life.

"*Turandot*" was a revelation to Melyssa. Like many Brits she associated opera with mystery, as something for the upper-class in London, not quite on the wavelength of a Bristol girl from a black household. She had heard of the big names of recent years like Boccelli, Pavarotti and Bryn Terfel and, of course, Emilio Monza, and she did like individual arias when she heard them on CDs of much-loved hits, or sometimes on radio, but had not been to Covent Garden or anywhere else to see a complete work.

In that warm Italian night, with an enthusiastic audience calling '*Bis! Bis!*' over and over again to receive another encore of some special aria that took their fancy, Melyssa saw for the first time how vitally dramatic, warm and basic opera really was. These hundreds and hundreds of people: children, grannies and tough-looking young men perched around her in the vast amphitheatre, were not the drawling aesthetes of popular imagination sitting upright in evening dress at Glyndebourne or The Royal Opera House. For the audience at Torre del Lago "*Turandot*" was a show, no different in its concerns from a TV soap – but so much more beautiful. She realised with a start that she did know the work, or part of it, as soon as "*Nessun Dorma*" began. It received huge applause. Emilio whispered in her ear,

'It always does. Long before the World Cup back in 1990, we Italians knew it was one of the world's greatest tunes. Even though I was only six then, I could sing it.'

As the great story was played out, the Chinese domes and roofs melting into the night sky as the final chorus swelled over the lake, the whole amphitheatre rose to give a standing ovation. At the end of that, after flowers had rained on the soprano, a small, fizzy man came on stage with a microphone.

'*Silenzio per favore, signori e signore!*' he howled. '*Stassera abbiamo fra di noi il tenore conoscuito in tutto il mondo! Emilio Monza! Eccolo!*' He pointed dramatically towards Emilio and Melyssa and a bright spot from on high picked Emilio out in his dazzling white attire. There was thunderous applause and shouts of '*Bravo! Emilio! Emilio!*'

'*Venga qui, per favore, Signor Monza. Si, si, venga....,*' cried the little man, making beckoning signs to Emilio.

He turned to Melyssa with a quirky grin, as if to say: What can I do? If they must have me, they must! Melyssa wondered whether Emilio had worn his white suit in anticipation of such a moment, for he radiated light and energy as he stepped on stage into the lights.

'*Nessun Dorma!*' shouted the audience.

Emilio smiled and went over to shake the hand of the tenor who had sung it that evening. The two of them came forward, and Emilio bent down and spoke to the conductor in the orchestra pit. During the ovations, musicians had begun packing up, as they do, and the pit was thinning out. The conductor laughed something back. Then, accompanied by part of the orchestra (those who remained and who probably knew it by heart) Emilio and his fellow tenor gave a spirited rendition of "*Non ti scorder di me*" which brought a gale of clapping and shouts. The other tenor then retired gracefully and Emilio performed "*Nessun Dorma*". Even Melyssa's untrained ear could tell that he sang with greater purity, mastery and sweetness of tone, and with a vibrating volume of passion, which far outshone his colleague's previous rendering. At the end of the song, the whole cast of *"Turandot"* surrounded Emilio, clapping and smiling. None, even the tenor who had starred in the work, looked sour or put-out; such was Emilio's effortless superiority and popularity.

At that moment, Melyssa realised two things she had not properly considered before. Firstly, she had not until now heard her lover sing in front of an appreciative audience and heard their worship of him. Secondly, she, Melly Mosengo, had caused this demi-god to rush to her Bristol suburb out of love for her. The responsibility and the magic of these revelations brought home to her how serious and important was her new-found love and her responses to it.

As the Porsche swept them back to the villa at Monte Bulciano, Melyssa prayed that the Contessa would be in bed. She was, and the house in darkness, save for a table-lamp left on by Sidney.

'Oh, Emilio! What an evening! What a day! I – I have never known such a wonderful day!' Melyssa cried, stepping forward into his arms.

He took her to him with authority. The thought of how he had swayed that great crowd acted as a stimulant to Melyssa and she felt herself diving into him, like a swimmer in the pearly seas.

They lay on the divan under a plate-glass window. Out on the Med, lights twinkled. Above, the stars burnt in the velvet dark. Melyssa felt as open as the sea, and he lay upon her as light as the sky. Memories came back to her of his tanned skin, the curly hairs of his body, his hard muscles. That day on the yacht had become part of her deeper dreams, and at the recollection she began to burn and ache.

Emilio made love to her sweetly, tenderly, with an artist's care. He did not again display the savage carnal urgings he had shown on the yacht. Looking back, Melyssa could not remember when she had stepped from her flaming dress, nor when he had turned from white to muscular dark – yet, undressed they were, turning over under the constellations.

Emilio spoke to her in Italian, spoke endearments and gave soft sighs. She, as the first delicious waves of hot sensual pleasure burst upon her, uttered wordless moans and a torrent of gasping breaths. Never, when it came, had she experienced such a blissful climax as this.

Melyssa was one of those girls for whom the place, the time and the emotions have to be right. Emilio's earnest words of commitment to her in Bristol had made their mark. She knew, without being able to translate the words he poured into her ear, that he was doing far, far more than satisfying, at last, the raging desire for her which had consumed him since their first meeting. Trust, unselfishness and gentle giving needed no language other than that of hands, lips and eyes.

So Melyssa's magic night ended in the equal magic of a million bursting stars deep within her body. If, as she passed into sleep after she had been led by Emilio up to her room and laid upon her bed, part of her regretted not glimpsing again that darker, primitive man she had provoked aboard the *Buona Fortuna*, it was a regret which could not allay the wild singing of her flesh and her heart as she lay folded like a bud in tingling slumber – once more under her Emilio's roof.

BETRAYAL

Next morning Melyssa woke with a guilty start. The tower and its theatre!

I must not presume on my relationship with Emilio, she told herself as she was getting dressed.

Days had been wasted in her wrangles with Bertini and then her flight home. But before she had decided she could not stand any more, she had put in a lot of work on her computer projections, had, with T-ray's help, contacted suppliers in Turin and Genoa who had guaranteed supplies of specified furniture and décor, had double-checked dimensions, hidden details and the radio mike equipment and the programmable LED lighting – vastly expensive, but necessary as tungsten-halogen was gradually being phased out in modern centres of performance. She had also, since the information she had gleaned about wind-farms in Tuscany, got T-ray to do research and to check that the hilltop at Borgo was not scheduled for compulsory purchase. He had texted her to say it wasn't, thanks to the proximity of the little town, whatever might be the case across the agricultural land which was owned by Loredana.

She felt ready – Bertini or no Bertini. She brushed out her corona of fluffy hair, pausing only to gaze in the mirror at her strong, well-proportioned body that had, so wonderfully, given her and Emilio such pleasure during the night.

She slipped on shorts and a T-shirt, finding herself smiling as she did so. She knew she was a girl who had discovered something about herself, a huge amount in barely forty-eight hours. Knowing that Emilio found her beautiful and desirable had the effect of making her want to flaunt her body, rather than cover it. Melyssa, like so many girls, was a lot more fastidious and innocent than she appeared from her tough exterior. Whatever her private sexual doings – and they had been completely private for more than ten years – she was shy about sexuality in public. Last night, she understood, had been the first time she had experienced the joy of sex with a man. Angelo and poor Brian had never counted.

With her laptop and her designs in her briefcase, she went down to meet Emilio. In the Porsche they set off for the Tower, Melyssa a little wary of seeing Bertini again. She need not have worried. With *"Il Boss"* at her side, Bertini was forced to concede that she had done all that a designer could do, and professed himself impressed as the materials had been delivered. He himself was now in direct touch with T-ray in Battersea, and no doubt this man-to-man contact had made a difference.

So a week, then another, slipped by and the theatre interior grew complete. The school had been ready for some time and was receiving final touches of paint and décor. Beds and bedding for its small dormitory were the last to arrive. Melyssa and T-ray had dealt with classrooms, kitchen and refectory already.

Then – as the late summer began to be more autumnal, and after a three-day visit from T-ray – Emilio became rather mysterious at the site. At the end of a hot but cloudy day, he informed her that much of her work was done, and that she might like to take a bit of time to relax: to swim, perhaps, to lie-in at the villa, to take a look at some of what Lucca and Pisa had to offer. It would be marvellous, he said, if he could accompany her – almost like a tourist.

As things had been going so well, she gratefully accepted the suggestion that they might slacken off a little. Even at the villa, matters had been less strained than earlier in the summer. Loredana was still there, but, breakfasting in bed as ever, she saw nothing of Melyssa in the mornings. After the evening meal, she would go to her room to watch TV, having drunk too much, as ever. Sidney was as easy-going and cryptic as usual, but he too seldom foisted his company on Emilio and Melyssa. Melyssa still had the bedroom she had occupied since the early days at the villa and, after quietly suggesting it, Emilio visited her on most nights before going to his room to sleep, for Melyssa's bed, though fine for love-making, was too narrow for two to be comfortable. Sometimes then, the lovers consummated their desires, but on many occasions they lay side by side and talked.

Emilio told her about his boyhood. He had had a tough upbringing. His father, Giovanni, had been a disciplinarian, he and his sister were often smacked. Thery were not well-off. Business dealing with farm equipment had not prospered when Italy joined the EU. Emilio's mother, Mona, was quiet and did as she was told, and what was expected of her. It had been rather tense when family meetings took place, for his father's sister Gloria had married a very rich Count, and the oldest brother, Frederico, Raffaello's father, was a lawyer with a big practice in Florence. It had been he who had paid for Emilio's training as a singer.

In her turn, Melyssa told him of her time in Bristol at school, her Art and design studies, her time teaching, hers and T-ray's struggles and ambitions, the support her mother and father had given her. She even touched on her brief affair with Brian, feeling it would be honest to tell Emilio everything.

Once she heard about his strict Catholic upbringing, and how, although he still believed in God and the teachings of Christ, much of his early assumptions and guilt had ebbed away, leaving him happier. He touched too on the world-wide decline in respect for the Catholic church after the abuse scandals among priests, although he respected Pope Francis greatly.

She, in turn, spoke of Abraham's low-church Presbyterianism, his strong belief in the Good Book and the family's regular Sunday worship. She too had modified some of her beliefs about sin, agreeing that some of both their religions' teachings were inappropriate now everyone had so much more understanding about science and human needs.

After one of these conversations, which she valued enormously because they were a sign that they something more between them than just sex, they had made love on her narrow bed, slowly and gently, taking a long time for each of them to reach their orgasms. When Emilio slipped back to his room, he left her utterly happy and fulfilled. Everything was just perfect!

Next morning her window shutters woke her with an agitated rattling.

She looked out of the window, expecting to see, as she had seen every morning she had been at the villa, the vivid blue of the sea and the bright sparkle of morning light coming over the mountains to the east. Now, however, the sea appeared dead and grey, sluggish under a heavy bronze sky. Immediately she had let the air-conditioned atmosphere escape, she realised how hot it was. Not yet ten in the morning and it was baking and humid. A storm was coming up.

She went downstairs.

'Emilio,' she called.

She was particularly desirous of seeing him that morning. Thinking back to the night, she felt her breath come in a gasp, as though still in a state of arousal. She longed to catch his eyes travelling up her legs, pause, and then take in her breasts and neck. She longed to smile into his face, to kiss him good-morning and to feel the shiny, even pressure of his teeth against her tongue.

'Emilio....?' She called again.

The house remained silent. O, Emilio, she cried inwardly, desperately, I need you so.

She crossed the marble-flagged hall as old Ada Pratesi came out of the kitchen door with a tray of coffee, *pane scuro*, butter, preserves and fruit.

'*Buon giorno, Signorina,*' said Ada, and gestured to Melyssa to follow her to the terrace where breakfast was usually laid.

'Where is....er, I mean....*dove* Emil – um, Signor Monza?' stammered Melyssa.

'*Poh! Non c'e, Signorina,*' shrugged the old woman. It was clear that she had no idea where "*Il Boss*" was. Melyssa felt that Ada did not wholly approve of the eager way she was asking after him, nor of her shorts and tight T-shirt, nor having to provide breakfast so late.

Melyssa thoughtfully ate breakfast alone. Goodness, how heavy the air seemed today. From the villa behind her came not a single sound. In fact, it seemed to Melyssa's ears that the whole valley leading to the sea was rather quiet. The normal whirring of three-wheeled motocarts going up to the vineyards and the rush of cars and roar of the buses from Lucca were missing.

She wandered back into the house after making a poor breakfast. She began to feel an unhappy self-pity. Has everyone forgotten me? Where is Sidney? And, more important, *where* is Emilio? Perhaps some early drama had occurred over at Borgo? But then surely someone would have awakened her? And where was the Contessa? Normally an early riser, Melyssa was up long before Loredana, but this morning, now that it was getting towards eleven o'clock, she had expected to have seen her. Even the Contessa's company, she felt, would have been welcome. But then it occurred to her that some things are worse than solitude, and the Contessa's company was one of them.

Melyssa sighed as she paced the not terrace.

Could they simply have gone down to the beach, or to the marina? Perhaps they were on the yacht. But Melyssa shook her head. No, surely if they had gone down to the harbour they would have left a note with Ada.

As the idea of a note popped into her head, she ceased to moon idly round on the terrace and went back in to look for a piece of paper pinned up. She felt rather cross as she did so. Really, they might have been more considerate and have woken her, rather than swanning off leaving nothing more than a message – if there was one.

'How am I supposed to get down to the bloody yacht?' she murmured to herself.

She had succeeded in persuading herself, by this time, that they were at the marina, even though the merest glance out of the window might have told her that it was not going to be a good day for going out on a boat. Off to the north-west the sky was almost black.

Rather to her surprise, because she had not really believed that there had been a note left for her, she spotted a message at last, pinned by a paper-knife to a grapefruit on the table in the dining-room. It occurred to her that had she breakfasted there and not on the terrace, she would have found it an hour ago. She tore it open and began reading.

Dear Miss Mosengo, (it began)
I'm taking the Bentley in to the garage in Via Reggio for its service – so you won't see me for the rest of the day. I guess you know what arrangements have been made for the day. I don't know what everyone's up to, but then who tells lil' ole Sidney anything? Emilio and the she-devil went off early in the Porsche. The boss doesn't expect to see you until this evening. I presumed you knew about this; I didn't like to wake you. I peeped in at 8.30 but you looked like Sleeping Beauty. Aw, too beeeoootiful to jerk you awake!

Have a nice day (as those barbaric Yanks say, so I've heard),

Your devoted Sidney.

Melyssa, irritated by the note's silly flippancy, so typical of Sidney, read it yet again, quite robbed of breath by the information in it. Emilio and Loredana? Together? Gone off in the Porsche? Gone off early? Where to? And *why*? And why the *hell* hadn't Emilio said something to her?

The unanswered questions tumbled through her mind, Crumpling the note, she felt for the chrome and leather arm of the Albrizzi chair which stood at the head of the table, and lowered herself into it. The leather felt warm and sticky against her bare legs. It was unworthy and, yes, unfounded, but all Melyssa's earlier misgivings about Emilio and Loredana shot back into her mind. She clenched her hands on the sides of her seat. Oh God! How would she cope if she lost Emilio now? Her body, still conscious in nerves and flesh of the delights of the night before; her mind already aching for the next night to come – she burnt to be reunited with him, to see him, to kiss him. And now this news.

Ada Pratesi came bumbling into the dining-room, a large wicker basket on her arm and a fan in her hand. She stood over Melyssa, breathing heavily, fanning herself, and in her limited English explained that she was going out. She seemed curiously put-out at having to do so, which struck Melyssa as odd.

'Puh! *Oggi* – today – ees impossible to find *pompelmi*,' she snorted.

'*Pompelmi?*' said Melyssa. 'Oh, yes, grapefruit.'

'Si, si, gratefood. But *La Contessa* she say: "You go and find". I not find on *Ferrogosto*. No shop on *la festa*….' Muttering, Ada left the room.

'Ada,' called Melyssa after her. '*Dove il Signor Fratesi?*'

She had asked where Ada's wrinkled-cheeked husband was because she felt a peculiar reluctance to be left on her own.

'Oh,' replied Ada. '*Oggi*, on days of *la festa*, 'e always go up to *il poderino.*'

Melyssa sunk back on the chair. So old Pratesi was up tending his allotment in the hills, Ada was going shopping, Sidney was taking the Bentley to be serviced and Emilio and Loredana had gone out at dawn in the Porsche. Really, it began to look as if there was a conspiracy to leave Melyssa on her own in the villa. It was almost like one of those films in which everyone is got off the scene before…..

Melyssa rose. The sky was, if possible, darker and the heat was sticky and threatening.

She thought: I wonder if something's happened at Borgo at the theatre? It occurred to her now that it was extremely unlikely that Emilio and the Contessa should have gone out to the yacht in the harbour on a day which promised a terrific storm. Perhaps Emilio had had some bad news about the installation of electrical equipment on the site. Now that Melyssa felt a proprietorial interest in the Tower Theatre and the school, as well as a professional one, this thought made her feel alarmed. Oh, please let nothing happen to the project – to my theatre, she cried to herself. It would be so ironic if she had come back and done so much work to find that the place had been in an earthquake, or, or…..

Why had no one spoken to her that morning? What did they expect her to do?

She had wandered irresolutely into the marbled hall. A glance at her watch told her how much of the morning had slipped away. I've done nothing. Nothing. But then what *can* I do?

She stood near the hall doorway, the flags of marble cool under her feet, and decided she must make up her mind. Then, out of the corner of her eye, she caught a movement on the terrace.

She was about to dart forward to greet whoever it was, hoping it was Emilio returning, when she changed her mind suddenly. Stepping into the house from the terrace were three men. Melyssa saw, at a glance, that they were young, two wearing dark t-shirts, one a black leather jacket. They were looking about them, but their eyes had not fallen on her. To her horror she noticed that the jacketed one was carrying a short, black cosh.

In very careful silence she retreated back into the hall and flitted down to Ada's kitchen at the rear of the villa. She realised that she should ring the police, and her hand went to her phone in her shorts' pocket. But what number? What could she say? She knew the Italian for "Help", but was not sure she could give whoever answered the right address. And it would be too late. She would be heard.

Assuming at first that the three young thugs were burglars – gypsies, perhaps, like those who begged from tourists in the Florence streets – she thought that she would be safe if she kept clear of them. They might steal her phone, but their intention must be to root through the house.

Then she heard one of them laugh, and the laugh was followed by a taunting call which froze her blood.

'*Signorina* Mosengo. M-o-s-e-n-g-o. You come out where you are.'

She couldn't move.

These were no burglars! For some unexplained, nightmarish reason, they knew her name. They were here to find her!

'*Signorina.* Don't be foolish…..' came the voice.

Melyssa darted into the kitchen and grabbed at the door to the outside. Ada had locked it. She spun back, her eyes wide, her nostrils dilated with terror.

'Bitch *straniera.* You no play games.' The voice was now harder and rasping. Its playfulness had vanished.

There was the sound of something smashing in the hall. There came a laugh.

'*Stupido!*' said another voice.

'You look upstairs, Giancarlo. *Io al cuccina.*'

Melyssa grasped what was said. She knew the Italian for kitchen. As footsteps came towards her, she darted behind the kitchen door and stilled her rapid breathing.

The kitchen door was shoved open. Melyssa glimpsed a jacket and a thick neck pass her. There was the sound of a rattle as Ada's pantry door opened. The figure went in to it. Melyssa, on tip-toe, crept out of the kitchen. Ahead of her the long marbled hall ran across to the main door. Upstairs she heard doors opening and closing. She whisked down the hall, gliding silent as a breath, towards the door to the outside.

In a second she was through and racing round to the outbuildings. She determined to hide out of sight there for as long as it took for the men to discover that she was not in the villa. As she ran into the garage, she remembered that Sidney had taken the Bentley for its service, and that Emilio had got the Porsche. There was nowhere to conceal herself.

As she stood, uncertain, she heard a shout from the house. They had discovered that she had run from the villa. Wildly, she stared round the garage buildings. Of course! The motorbikes! She nipped round into the low red-roofed sheds where Emilio's prized bikes lived. All were there. The massive GoldWing was behind the Norton. Melyssa thought she would stand a good chance of not being discovered if she squatted behind and partly under that huge machine. Surely no one would look between the great fairing and the shed wall.

As she was about to squat, two voices came more clearly. They were coming out to the garages! Melyssa abandoned her plan to hide behind the Honda and quickly darted, ducking as she ran, so that the low wall would conceal her, to the driveway behind the vehicles' buildings. Then she gave a gasp.

The Porsche was there!

Its convertible roof was folded back.

Sidney had told her in his note that Emilio and Loredana had gone out in it. Why had he written that?

And why was it not in the garage?

Surely Emilio would not have left it outside with its roof back on a day which looked so stormy?

More pressing than deciphering those unanswerable questions was the need to get away. Melyssa crept to the Porsche's door furthest from the building and got inside. Thank God, the touch-keys were in the cup-holder. Emilio's boast was that in this quiet part of Tuscany people were so honest there was no need to fasten doors and lock them. She had seen Emilio leave the Bentley with its keys aboard. Giving thanks for his belief, she pressed the power button. The engine roared into life. Thanking God for her first, admittedly not entirely successful, drive in this car, she shoved it into gear and aimed for the open gates onto the road. In the rear-view mirror she glimpsed a T-shirted man running, his mouth open and calling. The Porsche roared down the short drive. She turned left to head towards Borgo. Three running figures came to a stop in the road behind her.

Nothing in her previous driving experience had prepared her for her wild journey to Borgo. Convinced that her pursuers would be on her track, she careered the convertible onto the Aurelia; she had no money to pay for the autostrada toll, and little nerve to take the Porsche onto the that fast road, so, with her hair fluffed out and the wind in her face, she rushed between the flashing trees. Inside her, overcoming her astonishment that she was doing this, a spasm of worry about Emilio began to beat.

After a few kilometres she began to notice how little traffic there seemed to be, but apart from registering, she did not yet understand why.

As the Black Tower came into sight through the rushing foliage of the tree-lined road, heavy rain-drops began to fall, and a jagged fork of lightning cut the dark sky ahead. Above the car's engine, Melyssa heard a deep boom of thunder from the hills.

Pulling in, she began the task of getting the convertible's roof closed. While further drops fell, she looked for a handle to pull it back, but found nothing. It then dawned on her that the hood would probably be electrically controlled, so she gazed at the many little switches and symbols on the car's dash and panel. There was another menacing rumble and this seemed to spur on her intelligence. She pulled open the glove compartment on the passenger side, found the car's handbook in it, whipped it open and found a page about opening and closing the roof. She now knew which control to manipulate, and did so. She was just in time; as the hood clicked over her the rain started to fall in torrents.

Peering through the whisking wiper blades, she drove up the familiar road to Borgo San Martino and swerved round in front of the Tower.

The work-site was empty.

Leaving the Porsche, Melyssa splashed through puddles and gazed at the school and the theatre. There were no trucks, no sign of workmen, no sign of Bertini's Lancia. *Il Torre del Purgatorio* stood dark and sinister behind the bulk of the new theatre. Melyssa dashed the water from her eyes, and shook her fluffy hair. The downpour had ceased for the moment, but the sky was, if possible, darker than ever and, as Melyssa gazed up, two savage bolts of lightning struck the hillside above the school, and then a further flash seemed to play around the dominant column of the Black Tower. It was so like one of her dreams that she was shocked into stillness.

Like one awakening from a deep sleep, Melyssa's brain began to work. *Ferrogosto!*

Ada had said that today was *Ferrogosto.* It's August 15th and the Feast of the Assumption – one of Italy's greatest public holidays!

That's why the theatre site is empty! That's why Ada was complaining that she would it difficult to find grapefruit; the shops were shut. That's why the roads were so quiet. But, thought Melyssa, how did Sidney expect to get the Bentley serviced, as his note said he was going to do?

Just as the thought of Sidney flashed into her mind, she blinked twice. Why, there was the Bentley parked in the lee of the opera school's hall, its bonnet wet with rain!

With a physical jolt of realisation, Melyssa realised that the American had lied to her all along. He had lied about the Bentley, and he had lied about the Porsche. He must have lied about Emilio and Loredana too. Why, was it possible that Loredana had deliberately got an unwilling Ada out of the house on a quest for grapefruit? Someone had arranged everything so that Melyssa would be left on her own just at the time when…..when the three young men, one carrying a bludgeon, came into the empty villa looking for her.

Oh, surely Emilio would never, never have left her in danger. He could not know about these lies, these plans. Was he in danger himself? And where was he?

Melyssa had felt so confident of finding him here at the tower that she could not abandon her feeling that he must be nearby. Could there be some perfectly innocent explanation for all this?

There was another flash of lightning and a further roll of thunder. The sound reverberated from the tower's black sides. Just before the flash, Melyssa had fancied that she had seen a movement inside the doorway of the theatre at the tower's base. Instinctively, she darted back and crouched down by the Porsche, her knees touching her chin. With caution she raised herself to look through the car's windows and saw a figure stepping from the theatre. It was Sidney Gill. In his hand was a heavy wrench. With an odd gesture, as if finding it in his possession sickened him, he pitched it away. It clattered onto the ground. With his weak jaw clenched, he emerged further from the building, looking up at the shy. The rain was falling less heavily and the thunder had stopped. Clearly, the storm was passing away inland.

Melyssa, from her hiding-place, watched as he came out onto the driveway. He now had his back to her and was looking at the Bentley. She felt feverishly anxious to get inside the theatre. There was some secret there – something going on – and it was clear that Sidney had been up to something. Intuitively, she knew that Emilio was in danger. She now read every kind of sinister meanings into Sidney's actions. She wondered how long it would be before he turned and noticed the Porsche.

Strangely, she felt little fear of him personally; she could not believe that all his past kindnesses and good humour had been faked. She wanted to avoid drawing attention to her presence at the tower, however, until she had got to the bottom of what was going on.

She crept round the Porsche's front end as Sidney made his way to the parked Bentley. Under her feet were some fragments of tiling yet to be swept up and one of them cracked loudly as she stepped on it. She knew he had whipped round, but before he could take a step, she had dashed into the theatre and disappeared into the dark stalls seating.

She heard his exclamation as he noticed the Porsche for the first time.

'What the fuck…? Loredana?' he went on, 'Hey, what are you doing here?'

Melyssa ran up the centre aisle. The light came in fitfully from the foyer and the open doors. She scrambled onto the stage and slipped into the wings. She heard another shout from the back of the theatre, then running feet down the aisle.

'Who is that? I know you're in here,' came Sidney's voice, shrill and uncertain. 'Loredana, if that's you, come out and quit fooling around. What in hell's name are you doing here, anyway? What's happened at the villa?'

Melyssa huddled in silence.

'Hang it, you goddam bitch. I'll tell you now I couldn't go through with it. Is that what you're checking out?' hooted Sidney.

Melyssa retreated further into the wings until she came up to what was planned to be the stage manager's room. It was small, and the door hung open. Because some equipment including a PC would live in there, the door had a key in the lock. Melyssa grabbed at the door and banged it, then opened it again quietly. She crouched behind it in the gloom.

Sidney appeared in the wings. Melyssa took up a long bolt which was lying on the floor among other bits still to be cleared up. She then threw it round the door into the little office. Sidney darted forward with an oath and disappeared into the little room. At once, Melyssa leapt from her hiding-place, slammed the door, clutched at the key then turned it.

Immediately there was hammering and Sidney's voice, full of alarm, cried,

'Let me out, for God's sake. Are you doing it, then? Do you want me to be burned alive? Loredana, have pity. You can't do this to me, after all I've done for you! Please! Please! You can't just walk away now!'

Melyssa, to whom little of this made sense, leant against the door and crooned,

'I ca-a-a-a-n – and I ha-a-a-a-a-ve.'

'What? Who…. Who's that?' came Sidney's voice. 'That isn't Loredana, is it?'

'Guess, you liar,' said Melyssa.

'What! Is – is it *you*, Miss Mosengo?' gasped Sidney. 'What are you doing here? Did you come with Loredana? Has she squared you, or what?'

'Why did you think I was Loredana? What do you mean by "squaring"? What did you mean by saying you would be burnt alive if I left you locked up? Just what's going on? And where is Emilio?' She raised her voice, angry and puzzled. 'Tell me or I'll chuck away the key and you can burn or starve for all I care. TELL ME!'

Her shouting voice almost cracked with anxiety, with feverish worry about her lover. The thought that he had come to harm brought out a courage and determination that Melyssa had not known she possessed.

'Hey! No! No, no! Don't walk away! Look, I guess I'll let you in. There'll be plenty. Half my share, baby. Just turn that key....'

Before the imprisoned American could say any more, there was a sound of confused shouting from the open space outside. Melyssa, leaving Sidney locked in, ran back into the foyer of the theatre and peeked out. Standing round a grey estate car were the thugs who had chased her at the villa.

One of them called out, '*Contessa!*' and when there was no reply, they muttered for a moment or two then scattered: one into the school, one across to the Bentley, the beefy man in the leather jacket to the theatre. Melyssa backed into the dark and ducked down behind a row of stalls seats.

The leather-jacketed man stared round, then went back outside, to Melyssa's relief. She could see the grey car through the open doors and saw him take a large red tin from its rear. He then walked back to the foyer. With a gasp, Melyssa retreated again into the theatre's main body. She flitted onto the stage, went past the locked door behind which Sidney could be heard swearing, and continued backstage. Above this area the base of *Il Torre del Purgatorio* stood, its stones rising up a great height.

Her plans and Emilio's had always been to incorporate the tower's structure into the rear of the theatre so that its height might be utilised as a fly-tower up which sets and backdrops could be hoisted. Its massive base had been dismantled on one side before Melyssa's involvement, and huge supporting beams inserted in place of the great stones. Steps led down into the tower's basement. Emilio had thought this area would make for excellent props storage. Melyssa darted down these steps and waited, stilling her breathing.

Loud voices came to her ears. The three men were assembled in the auditorium. Then there was a silence, and a further call, this time from outside. Melyssa backed more deeply into the props area and, in the near darkness, stumbled over something soft. She fell to her knees. What she had fallen over stirred and groaned. Her heart pounded and she pressed herself against the wall, her fists clenched.

Another groan came from the figure on the floor.

Melyssa crept forward and peered down at it.

'Melyssa, Melyssa,' came a quiet voice. 'Oh, thank God. Help me.'

She gathered her senses and came close to the crumpled bundle. Again the voice spoke.

'Melyssa. It is Emilio. My hands and feet are tied. Let me loose.'

'Oh!' gasped Melyssa. 'Emilio, darling. Oh, my darling, who's done this to you?' She began fumbling behind his body at a leather strap knotted cruelly round his wrists.

'That cowardly bastard hit me in the dark,' muttered Emilio. 'On the head with something heavy.'

'Who? Sidney?' Melyssa remembered that Sidney, when she first saw him, had a wrench in his hand which he had thrown from him.

'Yes, Sidney, God rot him,' growled Emilio, suppressing a cry as his arms regained circulation. 'He got me in here and then turned on me. Am I bleeding?'

Melyssa peered with horror at Emilio's head. She tenderly felt over his scalp until her fingers came across a damp contusion.

'Ow! *Dio mio!*' gasped Emilio.

'Sorry, my love. There is a bad cut on your head and a swelling. The blood in your hair has dried.'

'Can you undo my legs?'

Melyssa felt down at his ankles and discovered roughly wrapped gaffer tape which Sidney had obviously found backstage. The adhesive and the hard edges had made his skin sore and red after she'd ripped the tape away.

His legs freed, he sat up, his back to the wall, and looked at Melyssa.

'What on earth are you doing here?'

Before Melyssa could explain, harsh voices, calling in Italian, came clearly to their ears.

'Who are....?' began Emilio.

'Sssh,' hissed Melyssa, kneeling down in front of him and putting fingers over his mouth. 'I'll explain why I'm here later. There are three guys up there and they were chasing me. They nearly got me at the villa. I don't know what they want, but I think Sidney is involved in that too. He lied to me about where he was going this morning.'

'He lied to me too,' whispered Emilio. 'He came early to me saying Bertini had texted him about a fire here at the site. He told me that a lot of damage had been done and that Bertini had insisted I come here and go over the costs and how much had been lost. God knows what his game is. But I'm going to find out. I'll have to wait until the *carabinieri* pick him up eventually, I suppose. He needn't think I'm going to spare him after this.'

'No, no,' said Melyssa, realising she hadn't told him where Sidney was, 'No need. He's here. I locked him in a little room backstage. I've got the key in my pocket. He's going nowhere.'

Melyssa felt a sense of pride for the first time in her resource. I'm like Granny Cavendish, she thought, fondly thinking of her mother's mother

– a child of the so-called Windrush generation who had arrived in England from Jamaica aged six, gone to an all-white school in a Somerset town, had worked tirelessly in the NHS, married an English electrician and had gamely and cleverly coped with money problems and prejudice and won through. Yes, I've got her DNA!

'Oh, my clever one!' smiled Emilio. He briefly took her face in his hands and kissed her. His lips tasted salty and exciting, and for an instant she clung to him in the semi-darkness.

A voice came down to them from the stage area. Then there was an answering laugh and a sharp smell in the air.

'What are they saying?' mouthed Melyssa.

'Something about who takes a red tin,' answered Emilio.

They stared at each other in the gloom.

'I saw one of them with a big red tin. It came from their car.'

'*Benzina.* Petrol,' articulated Emilio in Melyssa's ear.

'What are they doing?' she mouthed – although a second later she guessed.

'*Andiamo subito,*' said Emilio. 'We need to get clear, or to stop them.'

He took her hand and led her silently up the steps towards the rear-stage at the base of the Tower. They listened. There were at least two of the men in the auditorium and one on stage. They could hear the latter one's movements and a sloshing sound. 'No good. We can't get past them to go outside. We must climb. I have an idea.'

She felt him lift her against a cold metal ladder.

'Climb,' he mouthed in her ear. 'Climb quickly. You'll find that platform we designed about thirty feet up – remember? Wait for me on it. Keep against the wall. You might be seen if he looks up.'

Melyssa began climbing. Emilio, suppressing a hiss of pain as his sore ankles touched the rungs, followed her. Soon, they were on the fly-platform high above the stage.

'Look!' whispered Emilio. Beneath them they could see the man in the leather jacket. He was spraying liquid round the edge of the stage from a red tin. Melyssa put her mouth to his ear.

'That's the petrol smell! Who is he? Why is he doing that?'

'I don't know, but I'm stopping it now,' said Emilio. 'Here, take hold of this.'

Melyssa felt a thick rope in her hands.

'I'm going down first,' he went on. 'Pay this out slowly. You won't be bearing my full weight – the pulleys and the counterbalances will take that. But you'll be controlling my pace of descent. Imagine you are lowering a delicate piece of scenery for *"Rigoletto"*!'

Emilio grasped the fly-tower bars and pushed himself off into the gaping space above the stage. The rope descended silently. Beneath Emilio, the man with the tin had finished his task and had tossed the tin into a corner. A shiny trail of petrol snaked away towards the front of the stage. Its reek filled the theatre. Melyssa could see the thug fumbling in his jacket pocket as he prepared to walk away from the stage into the seating-area. She supposed he was looking for matches or a lighter.

Emilio jumped off the rope not six feet from him. The man spun round, his right hand still in his pocket. Emilio kicked out and caught him in the groin. He staggered back and fell heavily. Emilio followed and aimed a kick at his head. The man scrambled up and then tried to give grasp for grasp. With a sideways movement Emilio eluded the clutching hands and grabbed up the empty red tin. This he brought round in an arc, crashing it full in the thug's face. With a cry, the man keeled over and lay senseless.

There was a shout from the auditorium. Attracted by the noise, the other two, who had been on their way out, ran back into the theatre. They vaulted onto the stage, swearing. One dragged a flick-knife from his pocket and spat onto the stage before flipping it open. Emilio stepped away from them until he was under Melyssa's platform. He nearly skidded over on the wet petrol. With a laugh the youngest-looking man pulled out a lighter.

'*Cretino!*' cried Emilio.

'*No! No!*' shouted the man in the leather jacket. '*Benzina!*'

Realising the stupidity of igniting a flame in the benzine-rich atmosphere before they had got well away, the young man returned the lighter to his pocket.

Above them, Melyssa gazed down. None had looked up. The three advanced upon Emilio, the knife-man spitting on the stage again, shifting his weapon from hand to hand. Backing away towards the stage rear, Emilio seized the red tin again and flung it at the knife carrier. It caught him on the chest and he lost his balance. The knife dropped from his hand. Emilio kicked it away ahead of him down stage. It clattered over the edge. The two young men closed on him.

Above them, Melyssa grasped the metal cradle, which would be used to bring effects and scenes on canvas rolls up into the flies, and swung herself out from the securing blocks. The pulleys, uncontrolled by restraining hands on the ropes, whirled screaming. She shot down. The cradle crashed onto the heads of the young men. Emilio leapt forward to hold her as it landed, its fall broken by the human forms under it. She fell out of it into his embrace. All she could do was gasp with fright and relief. The drop was only thirty feet, and took only a second, but she had acted spontaneously without thinking that she herself might have suffered severe injury or worse.

'You could have been killed!' cried Emilio.

'I know. It was silly of me, but look!' She pointed to the underneath of the cradle. Two unconscious figures lay pinned by the metal cage. In truth, Melyssa could not have truthfully said she had actually planned to knock out the enemy; she had just leapt. But Emilio had no doubts.

'My brave, wonderful darling,' he said, drawing her to him again, his voice husky with emotion.

The youngest of the pinned men began to groan.

'Not dead. Help me tie them up.' Emilio jumped from the stage and retrieved the flick-knife. A few cuts at the fly-cable and he made six thongs. Melyssa tied the hands of one of the men under the cradle. He lay so still that she was fearful that he had been killed.

'Don't waste sympathy on them,' grunted Emilio, reading her thoughts. 'They would have burnt us to death.'

The man in the leather jacket was regaining his senses and was struggling to his feet, but Emilio grabbed his mane of hair and, forcing it back, warned him to be still. Melyssa tied knot upon knot round his ankles.

All three were now prone, one still unconscious.

Emilio took out his phone.

'I'm ringing the *carabinieri*. They need to come and get these three. God knows whether they'll be quick on *Ferrogosto*, but I'm not leaving them unguarded. Darling, would you go and release Sidney and bring him here?'

She took in his hard breathing, the flash of fire in his eyes. As a late reaction to the shocks and the excitement of the last hour, she swayed, inclining towards him with a slight, feminine gesture of appeal. He relaxed and held her in his arms.

'Darling Melyssa, I've asked so much of you – from the beginning; and you've never disappointed me.'

She felt tears of relief and reaction pricking her eyes. She clung to him.

'Now, go and unlock that viper Gill. If he tries to make run for it, let him go. But my guess is that he won't. He's not like these three.' As he spoke he looked down at the trussed-up thugs. All had now come to their senses. The leather-jacketed one struggled and spat out obscenities. Emilio knelt in front of him and took the man's stubbly jaw in his right hand.

'*Silenzio, furfante.* I don't want to hit a man who is tied up,' he said to Melyssa, 'But if I have to, I will.' He banged the man's head hard on the floor. There was a yelp of pain. Melyssa marvelled at his toughness and knowledge of how to act like a street-fighter. Somehow it was not to be expected in an operatic tenor. She realised that she knew only what he had told her of his upbringing and its circumstances.

'Go, *cara*,' he said gently.

Melyssa stumbled back into the dark rear-stage and jammed the key in the lock of the door behind which Sidney waited. He had long ago stopped banging and shouting. As the door swung open, she saw him sitting on the floor in the empty room, his head in his hands.

'Emilio wants to speak to you,' she said.

'I thought he would,' he muttered. 'Okay, lead on, sister.'

When they emerged back on stage, the three thugs were jerked to their feet by Emilio.

'You, Gill, help me get these scum into your little room. They can wait there for the police.' Speechlessly, he and Sidney, with Melyssa bringing up behind, led them, hopping clumsily, to the stage-manager's office. Emilio pushed them forward and they fell, cursing, to their knees. At a sign, Melyssa locked the door again. Then Melyssa, Emilio and Sidney left the building. Emilio found the number of the carabinieri in Pistoia on his iphone and rang them, crisply explaining the attempt to commit arson and the securing of the culprits. Melyssa, not understanding most of the rapid talk, nevertheless got the picture.

'Why don't you take a rest in the school?' suggested Emilio. 'I could do with a drink, and there's stuff to make coffee in that cupboard in what will be the common-room. You know the one.'

Melyssa did. She had had coffee there several times over the past fortnight. 'And you, Sidney Gill,' he suddenly shouted, 'you keep still. You're going nowhere yet. I want to talk to you.'

Melyssa did not hear what words passed between them as she made drinks and gratefully tidied herself up in the school buildings. She had noted the piteous fear in the American's eyes as she had turned away from him.

When she returned to tell Emilio that a hot drink was ready, the secretary had gone. She never saw him again.

Within the hour a police van had arrived. The three young men were hustled away. Emilio made arrangements to report to the *Questura* in Pistoia on the following day and to press charges.

Then Emilio and Melyssa were finally alone – for the first time – at the Black Tower.

'Now,' said he, turning to her with a smile tender and also quirkily cryptic, 'I can thank you properly for saving my life.'

The storm had rumbled away over the Carrara mountains and sunlight lit the tower.

'Come, my darling,' said Emilio, 'you have never seen the view from the top of the tower. Can you face the climb?'

'Can you?' Melyssa replied. 'Your poor ankles were chaffed nastily by that tape.'

Emilio laughed boyishly.

'I can face anything with *you* beside me, you fierce little kitten,' said he, with sincerity and evident joy at being with her.

'You do seem happy,' she said, as, led by him, they began the long climb up the medieval spiral which wound away up the tower. 'Especially after what has gone on here today. I know the crooks are now with the police, but who put them up to burning down all your work? I thought it was Sidney, but they were at the villa before they came here – and after me.'

'We're not at the bottom of things yet, I agree,' replied Emilio, 'but we will be. I think I'm happy because I have let go with one hand and taken hold with another. My future lies up these steps and my past below.'

'What do you mean? Do you mean that it's me you've taken hold of?'

'*Carissima*, that is exactly what I mean. I have been an idiot, but I've escaped the punishment I deserved for being blind. Do you want to know what that weak secretary of mine told me?'

'I knew he was up to no good when I saw the Bentley here. And he looked really scared after you had phoned for the *carabinieri.*'

'And well he might. He thought he was going to join our three friends in prison for attempted arson.'

'He can't have known what those guys were up to. He'd left you tied up, remember. And if they'd torched the place you would have been burnt to death.'

'Precisely. Why do you think he slugged me with the wrench?'

'But – but, surely he hadn't wanted you dead!'

Melyssa stopped climbing and paused, aghast that she could have so misjudged the smooth, friendly American. Emilio, a few steps above, came back to her. She leant in his arms and he pressed her to the rocky wall. The stone was refreshing to her hot skin.

'Yes, I'm afraid to say he did want me dead. He knew the theatre and the school were going to be torched, on a public holiday, with no one to report the blaze or stop it. But I had to go up in flames with the theatre, and he did hesitate to leave me to burn alive. That's why he cracked my head with the wrench – or tried to. He told me he lost his nerve and hit me a lot less hard that was needed. Sidney was not cut out to be a *mafioso.*'

'How terrible,' muttered Melyssa, almost feeling that she was in a movie script. 'And unbelievable.'

'All too believable. I misjudged him badly; very nearly fatally. I'd have simply burnt to death with a sore head, if it hadn't been for you….Super Woman!'

'What was his game?'

'As scripture tells us: *"Radix Malorum Est Cupiditas".*

'We had that in RE, I remember. The root of all evil is greed for money. That's it, isn't it?

'It all boils down to that,' said Emilio, beginning to climb slowly again. 'Sidney was not good with money. I employed him originally because his little English school in Sienna had gone bust. I felt I owed him a favour for what he done for my sister Angelina. He gave her a job back in 2019.'

'Your sister. Oh yes. She got smacked as you did. You hadn't told me her name, or what she was like.'

'You'd love Angelina, though you won't see her for a while. She married another Yank and now lives in Boston. Anyway, on with Sidney. Loredana fascinated him, of course. There's no snob like a Yankee snob; they love titles. He was a gambler, so is Loredana. Most of what cash she got from Dominico, the count, has long gone. And she and Sidney then conspired to get most of her land sold for wind-farming, as I have explained. Early on, after her widowhood, I had persuaded her to invest up here. But she had little confidence in my plans. Many, many times I've had to reason with her and persuade her that her money was safe. Recently, since your arrival, I'm sorry to say, she has grown obsessed with the idea that the theatre is not going to get finished, and even if it does, it'll never make a return on its costs. You see, she did not know then what you and I know now: that this hill-top would escape being used as the site of a wind-turbine. The tower is an ancient monument, and the town too close. She thinks if there were no theatre and no school, she could get a good price for the land up here.'

'Oh, Emilio – those meetings in her room. They were about all this?'

'Of course. Darling girl, I've already told you they were.'

'Yes, I know. You did. Yet I …..' What a fool, what a prat I've been!

'Let us climb on. Only another hundred steps and you will see the view.'

The spiral wound up. Melyssa and Emilio came out at last into the tower's top floor. The light was stronger, piercing through deep cut slits of windows, clearly built for defence. They went over to one of them that faced west. The view was astonishing: a huge panorama of sea, coast, Tuscan hills and little towns.

'Now we are here, I want to ask your permission to do something,' said Emilio.

'My permission?'

'Well, we are on your property, Melyssa. Can't really go ahead with a further plan without checking with the owner.'

'Honestly,' she grinned. 'If *you* want something, I do too.'

'Well, I was thinking of making this top floor into an office, for both of us, and with facilities, like a little flat, so if we had to be here late at night, we could just go upstairs. It would be wonderful to make love here up under the stars with all the world below us.'

Melyssa's arousal, never far away when she was with Emilio, at once tingled through her body.

'Oh, I *love* the idea!' she cried. 'I used to have so many dreams about the tower, but not that one.'

'To be in bed together after a performance…..'

'Worth the slog up,' grinned Melyssa, taking hold of Emilio's arm. 'Although after about three hundred steps we might be too tired to have sex!'

'Ah. But then I was planning to put a high-capacity lift up the back of the tower, on the side not seen from the carpark or the main buildings. Can't think how we'd get a double bed up here otherwise – let alone desks, filing cabinets, shower, loo, kitchenette….'

'Stop! I'm convinced! Let there be lift! And can I help in the design?'

'Well, that's my real point. I thought you and T-ray could have Calypso Designs Europe operating from Borgo right here. It would give the firm so much more reach.'

Melyssa's breath was taken away by the bold sweep of the idea. Her little Battersea outfit established in her own property in Italy! It was a thought of such bliss that it almost displaced that other blissful desire: making love with Emilio up here……

Emilio's face became serious once more.

'I have a little more to tell you, my lovely girl. Let's perch on this ledge and get our breath back. It's about that damned snake-in-the-grass, Sidney.'

'Yes. I want to hear about Sidney and what he told you.'

'Sidney told me that Loredana had hired those wretched *maleducati* to burn down the theatre. But worse – and I could hardly believe it of her – she engaged them to give you a little persuasion to leave Italy. That's why they were at the villa. After they'd roughed you up badly, they were to come here and destroy all that you and I had made. She thought the delay caused by complete destruction would cause those backers of mine to pull out. She told Sidney that if he could manage an accident to me, he would have half her money. She even went so far as to say she would marry him to make his share secure. And the stupid man fell for it.'

'No! My God, it's so melodramatic! It would sound unlikely in one of those Swedish film noirs!' gasped Melyssa.

Emilio sighed. It was clear that his secretary's duplicity had upset him; and as for his cousin's widow and her plotting....... Melyssa squeezed his arm. He sighed again.

'It's a terrible mixture of greed and jealousy, my love. And to think I trusted them. Well, no – I trusted *him*, I should say.'

'Where is he?' she asked.

'I am too soft,' he replied. 'He is a would-be arsonist, murderer and fraudster. Yet I feel he was led on by someone much stronger. So, I reminded him it was *Ferrogosto,* that I could not be pressing charges on the three stooges at the *Questura* until tomorrow afternoon, and that gave him a day to leave Italy. He gave me a look, almost of affection, and walked off down the hill. I expect he'll phone for an Uber, head for Pisa airport, and take his card to the max to get the first plane out, I imagine.'

'Loredana is a criminal,' said Melyssa. 'I know you once were sorry for her, but you – we – can't do nothing. Suppose she tries again?'

'I have an idea. Follow my lead, dearest. Let's head home.'

Emilio took the Bentley, and Melyssa took the Porsche, and they drove away in convey on the short journey back to Monte Bulciano. They came into the villa gates, parking next to each other on the drive. The door opened and the Contessa almost ran out, glass in hand. She gaped at Emilio and Melyssa, shaking her head in bewilderment.

'It's – it's you two? What are you doing here?'

'We live here,' said Emilio. 'Where else would we go?'

'But where have you been? At Borgo? Haven't you been with Sidney?'

'At the Tower? Yes indeed. Melyssa and I wanted to check a few future plans and their details. Great new ideas our clever girl has, you know.'

Melyssa, watching Loredana, added,

'We saw Sidney briefly. Then he left. Isn't he back here?'

Loredana's expression was extraordinary. With an eye furthest from her Emilio winked at Melyssa.

'Well, I could do with a drink,' he said. 'I see you've got yours. Come on, Melyssa, let's relax after our hard work today. It is *Ferrogosto* after all.'

They passed the Contessa and went into the villa. It was difficult for Melyssa to keep a straight face. When they had poured drinks and gone up to her room, Melyssa asked,

'What is the plan you've got to sort her out, then?'

'Just let's wait a bit. She can't figure it out at present. But I bet you there'll be a knock on the door tomorrow.'

That evening, Loredana did not appear for dinner. Ada was sent for to take her a tray to her room. Emilio and Melyssa lay, tired out, in each other's arms on her bed, until he retired to sleep, and she, locking her door, also fell into a long slumber. At breakfast there was no Contessa and just after midday there came, as Emilio had predicted, a long ring on the door bell.

Two members of the *Carabinieri* came in and asked to see the Contessa Frosinone. Ada called her, and she came downstairs with a strange mixture of fear and defiance on her face. The police arrested her, instructed Ada to pack a few things, and then took her out to their car.

Melyssa watched, amazed and glad. Emilio nodded his head.

'It was as I expected,' he said. 'Those three goons have told the police who hired them. I thought they would.'

When nightfall came, with Sidney and Loredana gone, Emilio took Melyssa to his suite of rooms at the villa. He had come to her room on several occasions, but she had never been to his. His small study and sitting-room were quietly decorated in white with gold touches. A desk of dark wood, a shelf with a Radio/CD player on it and two rosewood column loudspeakers were the only furniture. The bedroom had a king-size bed, simply covered with white sheets, a built-in wardrobe, a small table and a door to the bathroom. Again the colours were gold and white. Melyssa thought it was masculine and uncluttered, and immediately liked it.

As if divining her thoughts, Emilio smiled,

'I too can design a room, Miss Expert.'

'Oh, you!' she laughed. 'It is lovely and light.'

'I wanted you to like it because I wanted you to be at home in it. Always.'

With a grave gaze, he sought her eyes for a reflection of his own feelings. Her sensitive, full lips parted – in that sensual way he liked best of all her expressions – and her eyes danced with pleasure.

'You are asking me to marry you?' she asked directly.

'I've known since we met that I should be unsatisfied with any other woman, now and forever. If, darling one, you can see yourself as my partner, my lover, *mia amorata*, as we say, and it is what you too know is right, then yes, I am asking you to marry me.'

She had known since she had aroused the passionate side of his nature on the yacht that something in her spoke to his strongest desires. It was now not just the pull of attraction, but the recent strange events that linked them.

She could see that the romantic and fateful part of him that interpreted opera with such force needed to be stimulated by a relationship such as she could give him. The breathtaking sexual tension between them was as strong as ever, but they were now equals: she had known that she needed him, but today she had demonstrated her commitment, decisiveness and courage and had saved his life, and he needed her.

The sun lay fire-like on the Pistoiese hills. The room was filled with a rich glow. He opened a lower door in the desk to reveal a little fridge. From it he took a half-bottle of champagne.

'Corny, you might say,' he grinned, 'but it is to celebrate that we are still alive. We have come through.'

He entwined his arm about her waist as she sipped from her glass. She ran her tongue round her full lips. She knew that he watched for this. A gleam of excitement flared in the depths of his serious eyes.

'*Mia amorata*,' he whispered again.

His lips met hers and locked in a kiss sweet and searching. He took her glass, put it with his own on the little table, and let her surrender to his arms. The fiery sun made a dark corona of her hair, and he lifted his head back from her lips and sighed: a sigh of completeness, and a sigh of urgency.

She loosened the trousers and pants she was wearing. They dropped to her ankles, and she stepped from them. Immediately the tomboyish air she sometimes displayed vanished. He lifted her shirt, and regarded the uptilt of her breasts, her flat stomach and smooth thighs. When she felt the fabric slide down her legs her own senses flamed. Under his gaze, she leant back against the bedroom table, allowing her hand to drop between her legs. She savoured the familiar chemical change taking place in her body: the hardening of her nipples, the fire in her groin. Emilio was now naked, and her senses flared at the sight of him.

Emilio, guiding her to the bed, threw back the sheet and watched her lie down. The cool of the sheet was an aphrodisiac to her, and she stretched her long naked legs apart, lay back, her black fluff of hair spread upon the pillow, and slightly arched her back. Emilio looked down at her, his passion mixed with tender wonder.

'You are so beautiful,' he whispered. She extended her arms in a gesture appealing but child-like. She knew instinctively, as when she had parted her lips, that it was the right thing to do – to let him feel protective and also wanted desperately.

He lay by her, enwrapped. With an athleticism she hardly knew she possessed, fired by her sense of equality with him, she grappled with his body, the fingers of one hand digging into his back, the other grasping that fascinating hard part of him which she thought of, whimsically, as she admitted to herself, as a tough little creature which would soon be burrowing into its home. In his turn, he explored that home, stroking and gripping. When he entered her after their long fore-play, she gave a cry of joy. Soon her ecstasy came, moments after his own. It was the perfect love-making, as both knew; as wonderful as their last and so different from those hurried and silent moments in her room not far from the Contessa's and Sidney's. It was again rare and wonderful – and something that they would remember for much of their lives.

'Ah, my dearest love,' said Emilio some time later, as they lay together with the sheet spread over them, 'you must not return to the UK even for half a day before our wedding. I just want you with me always.'

Melyssa said nothing, but, inclining her face, pressed her lips to his lips.

'We are made for each other,' he breathed – as if to be re-assured. 'Do you not think so?'

'I know so, and knew from the beginning,' replied Melyssa. 'I'm not the sort of girl who gives herself to anyone, as I think you know. You just try to tear yourself away from me, and you'll see what I'm capable of.'

'You'll rush after me in a high-powered sports car, eh?' grinned Emilio.

'Well, I won't be swimming out to find you, in any case,' laughed Melyssa. 'If you want to get a bit of peace away from me, you'll have to maroon yourself out in the bay on your boat.'

'No, no! I vow never to set foot on the *Buona Fortuna* again without my wife by my side!'

He kissed her laughing eyes, her ears and the soft skin at her temples. Then he sat up, jumped out of the bed, and cried,

'Hey! I want you to listen to this! This is what we will open with. I have been thinking about this for months. Imagine: we are at the theatre's gala night, the curtains swing across – your curtains, yet to delivered, I admit – to reveal a detailed set. A voice is heard….. Well, just listen.'

He went into the other room and turned on the CD player. From the tall loudspeakers came orchestral music, and a girl's voice in supplication. Soon it was joined by another's: a tenor's, powerful and searching.

'That's you, isn't it?' called Melyssa.

'It is,' said Emilio, coming back to bed. 'Listen, darling. Just imagine it. You and I on the opening night of your theatre – the opera-house which you and I have made – and the music is pouring over us like a wave.'

The swelling duet rose and rose. Melyssa could hardly see Emilio next to her in bed. Only the eager shine of his eyes glittered in the August starlight. She touched his neck and throat and chest as the voices swelled; his chest, which produced these ravishing sounds.

He had brought the player's remote with him and turned the CD off as the song came to its end. Then he took her in his arms and lay down. She snuggled into him. It would be hours before dawn lit their faces and the faint noises of the awakening world came to their ears. Until then, forgetful of all but each other, Emilio and his Melyssa slept.

Loredana got two years in prison for inciting arsonists. Her hired thugs were given three years: for attempted arson and intention to commit bodily harm. Emilio gave his evidence at the *Questura,* as arranged, and later in the Autumn at court in Florence. He made no mention of the plan to murder him by leaving him in the burning theatre; some compunction, some slight familial feeling prevented that. Besides, as he had been rescued, there was nothing other than word-of-mouth evidence to support the accusation.

Emilio and Melyssa married in Bristol, from her step-father's home, and the reception at a large hotel was notable for the number of guests from the world of classical music whom Emilio knew. The event was covered in both the local papers and local TV and nationally in "The Times". What Abraham Mosengo thought of his step-daughter marrying a Catholic Italian, and what Angelina, Emilio's sister, who had flown over from America, and Emilio's mother, Mona, thought of him marrying into a mixed-race Presbyterian family was not known. All could see how much they loved each other, and that was enough.

The future would see a stream of cars inching up the newly widened approach road which led from the Aurelia to *Il Teatro al Torre* at Borgo. A uniformed figure would wave its arms to direct them to the car-park entrance. Where Bertini's dusty caravan had once stood, a pavilion of white and blue stripes would receive the guests. Passing through this pavilion, the guests would make their way up a dark-blue carpet to the theatre's entrance.

There on the steps to greet them would be the newly-appointed theatre manager, Luciano Foa, the Italian Minister of Culture, Signor Lombardi, the famous tenor, Emilio Monza, and the radiantly lovely Signora Monza. Signora Monza would be the topic of a lot of gossip. It would be rumoured, from not long after the theatre's opening, that she had met her husband in a strange and romantic adventure at the theatre which they jointly owned. Then and in the future, everyone would offer compliments to the stately young mixed-race English woman on her brilliant designs for this opera-house and, over the past few years, for other public buildings in Italy. She would now speak near-perfect Italian.

As the long line of smart opera-lovers would make its way through the pavilion onto the carpet, amused glances would be cast at the sturdy little boy who played with a toy car at Signor Monza's feet – a solemn-faced, attractive child with a touch of his mother's brown skin and her curly Jamaican hair, and his father's striking eyes. The tenor would reach down and sweep the little chap into his arms. The Minister of Culture would pat his head. A nanny – English, naturally – with freckled face and pink nose, would come down the steps from the cool interior of the auditorium to take the child home.

'Come, Giovanni,' she would say, and those guests nearest to the top of the steps would notice how reluctant his parents were to let him go. Each of them would hug him, his father delicately kissing his fluffy head. Emilio, when he would be born, would ask Melyssa if he might be named after his own father who had died aged sixty-six in 2020. His other names were to be Thomas and Raymond, a compliment to his uncle, T-ray.

The occasion on which all these people of the future were massing would be the third annual festival of Grand Opera in Tuscany – an event held for the preceding two years at *Il Teatro del Torre*, and which would be set to become the opener of the winter season of opera in Italy.

The pupils of the school would, in that near future, number thirty and be growing. A staff of five music specialists would be employed at the start, and a full curriculum offered in addition to lessons in piano, sight reading, singing and musical history – especially of opera. Melyssa would go back to her earlier job and, in addition to her design work with T-ray for Calypso Designs, would teach Art to the children at the school three times a week. She had always been a sympathetic and patient teacher with a good grasp of her subject and she would prove a success at her and Emilio's own little academy. The school's existence would prove to be one of the reasons why the Minister of Culture would attend the gala evening. The fame of *Il Torre del Purgatorio* and Borgo would reach Rome and the national press. It already commanded hundreds of thousands of followers on-line, and Emilio and Melyssa would be kept busy with their blog, their X twitters and their Facebook posts.

One by one the invited guests would file past their hosts and, before the last appeared, Emilio would slip away to don his costume and make-up.

'Good luck, darling. *Tanti auguri,*' Melyssa would whisper as he left her.

At length the curtain would swoop back on *"La Boheme"* or *"Rigoletto"* or *"Aida"* and another entrancing evening would begin.

'I have known Signor Monza for some years,' the Minister of Culture would say at the interval, smiling at Melyssa, 'and I think he has never looked fitter or more happy; nor has he sung so well as he does these days. You have been good for him, my dear Signora. It is not wise for a man to live only for his profession.'

Melyssa would smile back at the silver-haired politician. The line of guests thinned. Soon she would join the throng in the foyer and sip a drink. Before Emilio performed she would never be able to eat or drink much. Her eyes would sweep the pavilion area expectantly. There would come a whoop and a figure would run up the blue carpet.

'T-ray!' Melyssa would cry happily – as she was to do most years.

'Gosh!' T-ray would gasp – as he would do most years. 'Just made it as usual. You didn't think I'd miss it? Did I miss the last one? Where's Giovo? I suppose I *have* missed him.'

'Yes, you have,' would smile Melyssa, trying to sound severe, but failing. 'Really T, you always leave it until the very last second. Nanny's taken Giovo home to the villa. It is well past seven.'

'Oh, sugar! Still, I'll see him tomorrow. I've got him a neat present: a car that transforms into a hideous monster.'

Melyssa would take her half-brother's arm and squeeze it. T-ray's devotion to his nephew was famous in the family and Uncle T's visits would be eagerly looked forward to by the little boy. Now that Calypso Designs would have a base in Europe at Borgo, T-ray's appearances from London would be frequent. The UK operation would still be based in Battersea, and would have a dozen associates working on projects all over Europe and the UK.

Melyssa would smile at the Minister of Culture, introduce T-ray to him, and lead them both into the theatre. Before T-ray went in, he would, on this third year of the gala opening, take his half-sister's hand and pull her to one side.

'Just a word, Sis. You know you asked me to keep an ear to the ground about the Rio de Janiero job. Well, I've done it, and nothing came of it until last week. I didn't think it would, so it's great that there's been movement. But get this. I was contracting out some design work in Piccadilly with Brazilian Airways at their offices there, thanks to the Rio link, and an amazing coincidence happened. The exec mentioned something about liking opera when we were at lunch, so I told him that my brother-in-law was Emilio Monza, and he said: "Oh, I know someone he knows – a sort of cousin, I think – a Contessa Something-or-other", and I said, "Loredana Frosinone?" And he said: "Yes, that's right. She's getting married to my boss". Incredible, eh? So,' T-ray would say, 'mystery explained. No wonder Emil couldn't find her after she left prison. She's been living in Rio!'

'I'll tell Emilio after the performance. He was so angry with her for a long time. I think he worried too that she would go to pieces in prison. Trust her to fall on her feet and find an airline boss to look after her!'

'Yeah. Poor sap,' would grin T-ray.

The curtains would rise upon "*La Boheme*" and the audience would sit back and let the ravishing melodies pour over them.

As Emilio, in the part of Rodolpho, would come on stage, Melyssa would feel his eyes turn to where he knew she was sitting. He would play his scenes as though an invisible thread of gold linked his eyes with hers. Many in the audience would believe that he sang direct to them, but it was to his darling that he sang.

Melyssa was often to wish that this one final closeness with the man she adored were possible. Oh, that she were up there as Mimi, and that he sang those divine melodies for her alone. This would be, perhaps, her one secret unhappiness: that she could not penetrate the magic world of the stage and sing out her love for him for all to see.

And yet, she would think, this is *my* theatre – *my* work, and *my* designs are everywhere – and above us all is our special room in the Black Tower, and when these strangers are gone, and the story is ended, Emilio and I will go home to Giovanni and we…… Melyssa's face often flamed in the darkness of the auditorium as her thoughts would race to their bed and the intimacy of their love.

She would dream no more of the Black Tower. She would find herself thinking that whatever was in her that created those dreams had been exorcised. And at the thought of all her new-found joys, a warm wave of pure happiness would flood over her.

Melyssa, with sparkling eyes, would drink in her husband's and lover's matchless song and would let her mind dwell upon the bonds between them which would sustain and keep her happy her long into the future.

THE END

OTHER NOVELS BY SIMON POTTER from *Trans-Oceanic-Press*
Available from bookshops, Amazon and Witley Press Bookshop:

"Losing It All". 1960s London boys Anthony and Mike are fascinated by their grandfather's magnificent haunted Scottish house. When it becomes a school on the old man's death, Anthony teaches there. ('Hilarious and touching' *The Month.* 'Novels like this are the best sort of history' *BBC World Service)* ISBN: 978-1-9164295-2-9

"Dressing as Julia". (Global Book Award 2023) A shortage of girls for St Matthew's Catholic High's end-of-semester play sees Jem Clarke taking the part of Julia. His gay teacher and an older pupil become obsessed by him. When the play leaves New York for a Canadian summer school, lives are changed….. ('Has a feminine feel for teenage infatuation and a masculine sense of irony' *Susan Janni.* 'Finely written with a surprising plot' *Amazon review*) ISBN: 978-1-9164295-1-2

"Together Forever?" Mike is homesick in LA. He invests in a TV series and returns to London, but his insane ex-lover pursues him with a horrifying plan to keep them together. ('A well-observed page-turner', 'Humorous, shocking and bizarre', 'Remarkably intelligent' *Goodreads.* 'Riveting. It surprises and entertains on every line' *Amazon*)
ISBN: 978-1-9164295-5-0

About the author:

Simon Potter's published work includes history, fiction, memoir, literary commentary, technical non-fiction, poetry and articles for magazines on and off-line. He has written, adapted and directed nearly 70 plays and musicals for youth theatre. He lives in London, England with his wife, and teaches part-time, preparing pupils for Oxford and Cambridge and revising A Level English Literature at the Jesuit College in Wimbledon where he was Head of English from 1981 to 2002. He was awarded an MBE for services to education in Queen Elizabeth II's ninetieth birthday Honours in 2016.

www.simonpotterauthor.com

oOo